**Ashleigh thought her heart
was going to break . . .**

"What's wrong?" Ashleigh asked softly as she reached the stall.

"Holly's just had her foal," her mother said quietly. "A filly."

On the thick bedding near Holly's feet lay a long-legged foal—a very small foal. Her still-damp coat was the color of copper, but she had four white stockings and a snip of white at the end of her nose. She looked at Ashleigh from huge, dark eyes too big for her finely tapered face. The appealing look went straight to Ashleigh's heart. "She's beautiful," Ashleigh whispered.

"Sweetheart," her father said gently. "I don't think this little filly's going to make it."

"Can't you help her?" Ashleigh said in a small voice.

Mrs. Griffen's face was drawn and pale. "Maybe you should go up to the house."

"No!" Ashleigh said. "You can't just let her die!"

THOROUGHBRED

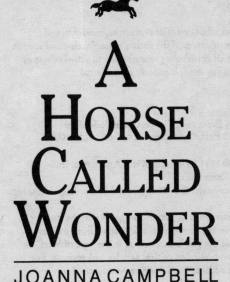

A
HORSE
CALLED
WONDER

JOANNA CAMPBELL

HarperPaperbacks
A Division of HarperCollins*Publishers*

This is a work of fiction. The characters, incidents, and dialogues are products of the author's imagination and are not to be construed as real. Any resemblance to actual events or persons, living or dead, is entirely coincidental.

HarperPaperbacks   *A Division of* HarperCollins*Publishers*
10 East 53rd Street, New York, N.Y. 10022

Produced by Daniel Weiss Associates, Inc.
33 West 17th Street, New York, New York 10011.

First printing: August 1991

Printed in the United States of America

HarperPaperbacks and colophon are trademarks of
HarperCollins*Publishers*

10 9 8 7

A
HORSE
CALLED
WONDER

FROM THE FRONT PORCH OF HER NEW HOME, ASHLEIGH GRIFFEN looked out to the rolling pastures and white-fenced paddocks of Townsend Acres. It seemed so strange to be here and know that this was where they would be living from now on.

The last few months had been the most horrible in Ashleigh's twelve years. First a virus had swept through her family's own small breeding farm, Edgardale, farther north in Kentucky. Five of their best broodmares and one foal had died. As if that hadn't been bad enough, her parents had made the sad announcement that their insurance didn't cover their losses. Edgardale would have to be put up for sale and the remaining stock sold. They would have to find work somewhere else. Luckily, they had been able to —as the breeding managers at Townsend Acres.

Ashleigh felt like crying just thinking about it.

Townsend Acres was as beautiful and well kept as Edgardale, with dozens of sleek Thoroughbreds romping in the paddocks. *But it isn't Edgardale,* Ashleigh thought, *and the horses aren't ours!* They all belonged to the owner, Clay Townsend, who Ashleigh was sure would be awful.

She banged her fist down on the porch railing. She was furious with her parents for selling Edgardale—she felt angry about everything!

Sighing heavily, she went back inside the house. Mr. and Mrs. Griffen were in the kitchen having coffee. They both looked tense and tired.

Maybe she shouldn't be so mad at them. They looked like they felt as bad as she did.

"Ready to go on our tour?" her mother asked. "Why don't you run up and get your brother and sister?"

Ashleigh went out to the front hall and up the staircase to the second floor. "Caroline, Rory!" she called as she reached the landing. "Come on, we're going."

When she didn't get an answer, she walked down the hall and into the bedroom she would share with her older sister. With her radio blaring away, Caroline was hanging some clothes in the closet. She was fifteen—three years older than Ashleigh—and incredibly neat. Already a line divided the room. Caroline's side was immaculate. On Ashleigh's side, boxes were piled near the bed waiting to be unpacked, and the bed was rumpled and covered with horse magazines.

Caroline turned from the closet. "I'm busy. And besides, I don't care about seeing Townsend Acres."

"I don't want to, either," Ashleigh said, "but we're going to be stuck living here. Aren't you even a little curious?"

"It can't be that different from Edgardale."

"It's bigger. Dad said they have their own training stable."

"So what? I'm sick of horses and everything to do with them! I'm staying here and putting my clothes away."

At that moment their seven-year-old brother, Rory, hurtled into the room. "I'm ready!" he shouted. He was too young to understand what had happened at Edgardale. His red-gold hair was sticking up all over his head, and there was a smudge of dirt on one of his cheeks. Caroline had the same red-gold hair, except that hers was perfectly combed. Only Ashleigh had their father's dark hair and hazel eyes.

Rory raced over and jumped up on Caroline's bed. Caroline screeched and grabbed an armful of clothes she'd been getting ready to hang. "Go jump on Ashleigh's bed!" she cried. "It's a mess anyway."

Ashleigh took Rory's hand, pulled him off Caroline's bed, and started leading him from the room. "Come on, Rory. The heck with her."

Their parents were waiting in the front hall. "All set?" Mr. Griffen asked. "Where's Caroline?"

"She doesn't want to come," Rory said.

"Caroline!" Mrs. Griffen called sternly. "We're waiting!"

In a moment Caroline appeared. "Why do I have to go? I want to get my stuff put away."

"You'll have plenty of time to do that later. It's time now for the family," her mother answered. "We're all feeling rotten about having to move, but we have to make the best of it. You might even enjoy yourself. Mr. Townsend has a son about your age."

"Does he?" Caroline said. "I didn't know that. Maybe he'll be in some of my classes at school."

"I think he goes to a private day school, but I know he takes a lot of interest in the horses."

Ashleigh noticed that Caroline looked a little less gloomy as she followed the rest of her family outside. Her sister had never been horse-crazy like the rest of them. Even when they were small, Caroline had loved clothes and used to dress up whenever she could. While Ashleigh had raced around on her pony, Caroline had sat in the backyard reading a book or experimenting with nail polish.

As they walked along the graveled drive away from the house, Ashleigh sniffed the scent of new grass— the famous Kentucky bluegrass, which wasn't blue at all but a very bright green. Leaves were sprouting on the trees lining the drive and paddocks, and the fences wore a coat of fresh whitewash. *If only we had come to Townsend Acres for different reasons,* Ashleigh thought.

Their father led them into the first of the long, well-lit barns. The barn smelled of horses and fresh hay. Normally, the smell was like perfume to Ashleigh. Now it only brought reminders of her last visit to the Edgardale barns when she'd said good-bye to her special mare, Stardust. She'd ridden Stardust from the time she was big enough to graduate from their pony, Moe. They'd spent hours and hours together jogging around the farm—and now Stardust belonged to someone else! Ashleigh felt a lump in her throat. She had to think of something else, or she'd start to cry. She looked into the barn at the bustle of activity.

Two young stable hands were busy cleaning the stalls, pitchforking the dirty bedding into wheelbarrows and hosing down the concrete center aisle. A man with graying hair hurried over and shook Mr. and Mrs. Griffen's hands. Ashleigh's parents had already met most of the regular staff when they'd come to interview for the job. Mr. Griffen introduced the man as Bill Parks, who kept an eye on the expectant mares.

"Pleased to meet you," he said to the children, then he spoke to Mr. Griffen. "We had a nice little colt born this morning. Maybe you'd like to take a look."

"We sure would."

Bill led them to a big, square stall. They looked over the halfdoor to see a fuzzy-haired, coal-black foal curled up on the straw. As they watched, his mother lowered her head and gently nudged him.

"He's been up and around," Bill told Mr. Griffen. "He's strong on his legs and is just taking a little rest now."

Ashleigh lifted Rory so he could have a better look. She loved the awkward little foals. At Edgardale she'd helped lead them to the paddocks when they were old enough to go outside with their dams. But today Ashleigh could hardly stand to watch.

"Oh, look," Rory cried, "he's standing up!"

The foal slowly unfolded his long legs from under his small body and unsteadily tried to rise. He swayed and almost toppled, but his dam nickered encouragement, and in a moment he got his legs firmly beneath him. He stood, feet braced wide apart, proudly looking at his audience and twitching his tiny brush of a tail in triumph. Rory laughed with delight.

"Hard to believe that bundle of legs is going to be a powerful racehorse one day," their mother said.

"I wish he'd stay little." Rory sighed.

"We'll see what we can do about finding you a real pony," promised his father.

"Like Moe?"

"Yes, like Moe." Derek Griffen rubbed his hand over Rory's tousled hair. "Well, we've got a lot more to see. I'll be in later, Bill, and look over all the mares."

Bill waved them off.

They continued down the line of barns and sheds. The late April sunshine was warm. Birds chirped in the branches of the trees, and occasionally a horse whinnied loudly from the pastures. They passed paddocks where the mares in foal were grazing. In other paddocks playful yearlings raced over the fresh green grass, kicking up their heels and frolicking.

In the stallion barn they met Tom O'Brien, the stud manager. He was short and stocky, and his blue eyes twinkled when he smiled. "The stallions are all out in their paddocks. Come and see."

Tom called out the names of the animals as they passed each paddock, then he showed them the farm's three prize stallions. "This is Fleetknight." He pointed to a coal black horse who was shaking his elegant head. "And that bay is Barbero. The next one over is Townsend Pride. He won the Kentucky Derby and the Preakness a few years back. He was born and trained right here."

Ashleigh could barely take her eyes off Townsend Pride. They hadn't kept stallions at Edgardale, and she was intrigued despite herself. He wasn't as big as the other two, but he was definitely the most beautiful. His gleaming coat was chestnut, shining like a brandnew penny, except for two white stockings on his front legs. His mane and tail were long, silky, and flowing, and he moved around his paddock with the grace of a ballet dancer.

7

"Why do you keep them in separate paddocks?" she asked Tom.

He laughed. "They say horses aren't very smart, but they sure can think of a lot of ways to get themselves in trouble. Especially the stallions. They'd be fighting with each other if we gave them a chance, so we separate them and keep an eye on them all the time. We don't want these fellows hurting themselves."

Ashleigh didn't think horses were as dumb as some people thought. You just had to understand them and get them to love and trust you—then they behaved beautifully. But she didn't have time to argue. Already her parents were leading them off on the rest of their tour. The farm was much bigger than Ashleigh had imagined, and after the quiet peacefulness of Edgardale, all the activity was a surprise and kind of scary. She glanced around nervously when they entered the training area. Even though it was Sunday, Ashleigh could sense the excitement and prestige of a famous racing stable.

Stable hands looked up as the Griffens passed. The hands were enjoying the nice weather, sitting outside on benches to polish tack and clean brushes. Others were walking sleek Thoroughbreds in the shade of the half-leaved trees. The horses all wore light blankets of green and yellow, emblazoned with the letters *TA* for Townsend Acres.

Mounted exercise riders left the stable area for the

track. Others were riding the exercised horses back to the barn.

"They're getting these horses ready for the racing season," Mr. Griffen explained. "Quite a few have already left for different tracks, especially the three-year-olds that are prepping for the Kentucky Derby. I know Mr. Townsend has several horses nominated—Townsend Victor for one. The colt did real well last year."

He showed them the two big barns for stabling the racing stock, with attached tack rooms and trainer's office. Another barn was for hay and feed storage, and there were large sheds to house the equipment used in keeping up the training track and grounds. At the far end of the training area was a long, low building where the help who lived on the farm had their rooms. Ashleigh knew that the Griffens were lucky—they had a whole house to themselves.

Inside the stables, the horses that had already been worked on the training track that morning were in their stalls being groomed. "Are any of these horses big stakes racers?" Ashleigh couldn't help asking as they walked past the stalls.

"I'm sure they are, but you'll have to ask Ken Maddock, the head trainer," her father told her. "He should be around somewhere. In fact, let's go look at the training ring. Remember, your mom and I won't be having anything to do with the training—only the breeding end, like we did before—" His voice dropped and for a moment he looked away. Then he quickly straightened his shoulders and led them on.

The training oval looked like a regular racetrack, except smaller. It was surrounded by low fences, with poles set along the rails to mark the distance and a starting gate positioned on one side of the track. A man stood on the outside of the rail. He had a stopwatch in his hand and was watching a horse and rider out on the track.

"That's the trainer, Mr. Maddock," Ashleigh's father told them as they paused to watch. The horse and rider on the track flashed by the half-mile pole, and Mr. Maddock checked his stopwatch. The rider slowed the horse, turned, and trotted back toward the trainer.

"Not bad!" the trainer called. "Better than yesterday. How'd he feel?"

"Good! Ready to go," the rider called back.

Ashleigh first studied the horse, another chestnut, then the boy in the saddle. He looked like he was in his teens, not much older than Caroline. He was fairly tall and thin and kind of cute. It was hard to tell much else about him with his helmet on, except that he was an awfully good rider. She wondered who he was. He didn't look old enough to be a regular exercise rider.

He rode his mount out of the ring at a walk, dismounted, and led the horse over to the trainer. Mr.

Maddock ran a hand over the horse's legs and nodded. "No heat. We'll try him over five furlongs tomorrow." He looked up, saw the Griffens, and lifted a hand in greeting.

"First day, eh?" he called to Mr. Griffen.

"Moved in this morning." Derek Griffen smiled. "Thought I'd take the family on a tour of the farm. You haven't met my wife, Elaine, who'll be working with me."

"A pleasure to meet you," Mrs. Griffen said as she shook the trainer's hand.

"And these are my children—Caroline, Ashleigh, and Rory."

The trainer nodded to the children and smiled.

"Nice ride," Mr. Griffen said to the boy holding the horse. "Nice-looking colt, too," he added to the trainer. "One of Townsend Pride's?"

"Yup," Maddock said. "He's one of our most promising two-year-olds. Brad's been working with him. You know Mr. Townsend's son, Brad, don't you?"

"We've heard of him, but haven't met. How are you, Brad? I'm Derek Griffen. My wife and I will be managing the breeding farm."

"Hi," Brad said curtly. He neither smiled nor extended his hand, but instead turned his back on the Griffens and finished his conversation with the trainer. "I thought we could try him from the gate tomorrow. What do you think?"

"Maybe," the trainer said. "We don't want to rush him. Take him back to the stable and have one of the grooms walk him."

Brad remounted and rode off. "The kid's pretty intense," Maddock said, apologizing for Brad's behavior. "And that's his colt. He's bringing him along himself."

Ashleigh thought Brad Townsend was just plain rude. Her parents would have had a fit if she'd acted like that. Was he trying to rub it in that they were just help, and he was the owner's son? Out of the corner of her eye, though, she'd seen Caroline perk up, fluffing her hair and giving a dumb smile. Ashleigh could have kicked her for acting like a jerk.

Ashleigh watched Brad ride away while her parents talked for a moment to the trainer. From the way he sat in the saddle, she could tell he knew exactly how good a rider he was. She felt like calling out, "We were owners of a farm, too, stuck-up!"

When they'd said their good-byes and were starting toward home, Ashleigh spoke up. "I don't think I'm going to like him."

"Who?" her mother asked. "Mr. Maddock or Brad? And you shouldn't jump to conclusions about people."

"Brad, and you didn't like him either. I could tell by the look on your face."

Her mother smoothed her expression. "Well, I've met more polite kids in my life, but you still shouldn't jump to conclusions. Maybe he was just preoccupied with his ride."

"His colt had better manners."

"Ashleigh," her father warned. "I think we're all feeling pretty frazzled and high strung. Your mother and I are going to go talk to Bill and look over the mares. You guys can either come with us or go up to the house. I noticed there's a pretty nice swing set in back of the house, Rory."

"I want to play with my trucks, but I couldn't find the box they were in."

"Look in the garage," Mrs. Griffen told him, "but I don't want you leaving the yard."

"I want to finish unpacking," Caroline said, "not watch him!"

"If Rory doesn't behave, send him down to the barn."

Caroline took Rory back to the house, and Ashleigh followed her parents to the foaling area. The barns brought sad memories, but she didn't want to go back to the house either. She didn't care if her clothes ever got unpacked.

While her parents talked to Bill Parks, she wandered around listlessly. Then one of the grooms came over to say hello. She had curly red hair and freckles and was probably about twenty, Ashleigh guessed.

"Hi, I'm April," she said.

"I'm Ashleigh."

April gave her a friendly smile. "It's hard coming to a new place, but you're going to like it here."

"I don't know about that." Ashleigh sighed. "We had our own breeding farm and had to sell it a couple of weeks ago. I can't get used to being here."

"What happened?" April asked.

With April sympathetically listening, Ashleigh found herself blurting out the whole story. She was surprised at how much better she felt just being able to talk about it.

"That's awful!" April cried. "You guys must feel terrible! I know I would."

"Yeah," Ashleigh agreed. "And now my parents have to work for someone else, and we all miss our place."

"If it makes you feel any better," April said, "this is a good place to work—good facilities, fantastic horses. Come on, I'll give you the tour."

April introduced her to the other foaling groom, Jesse. Jesse was muscular and blond, and he told Ashleigh he wanted to be a breeding manager one day. Then April showed Ashleigh the layout of the tack room and feed room, and asked Ashleigh to come along when she brought in the mares and foals for the evening. April told her the names of each of the mares. A lot of the mares had been given nicknames by the hands, and those were the names Ashleigh preferred. Lively, and Sparky, and Sad Eyes, and Three Foot, a broodmare who'd been injured in an accident years before and still walked with a slight limp.

The last mare April showed her was Townsend Holly. "Holly was a stakes racer in her day," April said, "but that was a long time ago. She's close to twenty and beginning to feel her years. But she's a good broodmare—what breeders called a 'blue hen.' Her foals almost always go on to be successful racers. She's carrying one of Townsend Pride's foals. This may be her last one."

Holly was a big chestnut, and Ashleigh suddenly felt tears in her eyes. Holly looked like Stardust! Holly's back had begun to sway a little from age, Ashleigh noticed, and her coat didn't have quite the smooth sheen of some of the other mares, but Ashleigh felt drawn to her like a magnet.

As soon as Ashleigh came to Holly's stall, the mare dropped her head over the door, gently nudged Ashleigh's shoulder with her muzzle, and whoofed soft breaths onto Ashleigh's cheek.

Ashleigh had sworn she wouldn't get close to another horse—she didn't want to be hurt again—but she couldn't stop herself from reaching up and rubbing a hand over the mare's soft muzzle. She scratched Holly's ears, then fed her a bit of carrot that April had given her.

"You want to be friends, don't you, girl?" Ashleigh asked. The mare bobbed her head, as if nodding yes.

"You know, I used to have a horse who looked like you."

Holly nickered and nudged Ashleigh, looking for another carrot. Ashleigh dug in her pocket and found one for her.

"She's nice," Ashleigh said to April.

"Yeah, she's an old sweetheart. She and Three Foot are my favorites."

They finally turned from Holly's stall and started back down the barn. Ashleigh glanced over her shoulder at the old mare, who still had her head over the door, watching Ashleigh. Yes, she looked a lot like Stardust, Ashleigh thought, and was just as sweet and friendly.

As she and April approached the stable office, Ashleigh saw an old man talking to her father and Jesse. He wore baggy clothes and a tattered felt hat. Ashleigh had seen him earlier that day near the training stables. He'd been one of the few people who hadn't smiled back when her father had waved hello. "Who's that?" she asked April.

"Oh, that's Charlie Burke. He used to be head trainer. Mr. Townsend retired him when he hired Mr. Maddock. He let Charlie keep his rooms because he didn't have anyplace else to go. Charlie's always wandering around, checking things out."

"He doesn't look very friendly," Ashleigh said.

April shrugged. "That's just Charlie's way. He doesn't like being retired."

As Ashleigh watched, the old man said something to Jesse, scrunched his crumpled old hat down further on his head, and left the barn.

Because it had been such a busy day, Mr. Griffen drove the ten miles into Lexington to bring home pizza for dinner that night. They all plopped down in the living room to eat off paper plates. The moving company had brought the furniture in and set it around the room, but the cardboard boxes holding all the Griffens' paintings, books, and knickknacks were still pushed into the corners.

"I don't know when we're going to find time to get everything unpacked," Mrs. Griffen said, reaching for a slice of pizza.

The others were all hungry and reaching for pieces, too. "Don't worry," her husband said between bites. "It can wait. And we'll all pitch in."

"But I want this new house to feel and look like home." She looked anxiously at her children. "What do you all think? Do you like it? Do you think you're going to be happy here?"

Rory had already spilled sauce down the front of his shirt. "I like it!" he mumbled through a mouthful.

"Rory, you know you're not supposed to talk with

your mouth full," his mother gently scolded. "What about you girls?"

"It's a neat farm," Ashleigh said. She could tell from her parents' faces that they were worried and were trying to be cheerful. She didn't want to tell them how homesick and angry she'd felt that morning. "I think it may be okay."

"Good," her mother said. "Caroline, you seem awfully quiet."

Caroline had been staring down at her plate. She shrugged. "It'll be all right, I guess." But she sounded depressed.

"I know it's hard," her mother said quickly. "We all miss Edgardale. Your father and I didn't want to sell it and move, but we didn't have any choice. This will be a new start for all of us."

Later that night when the girls were getting ready for bed, Ashleigh said to Caroline, "You don't like it here, do you?"

Caroline didn't try to pretend. "No. I thought it was going to be different. I thought we were going to be close to Lexington, but we're ten miles away! It's different for you—as long as you're around horses, you're happy."

"I miss Edgardale, too, you know, Caro," Ashleigh protested. "And you'll be going to Lexington every day for school, remember."

"Sure, but I'll have to take the bus home right after. I won't be able to stay in town and do any fun stuff!"

"Mom and Dad won't mind you staying late for things. There'll be plenty to do—probably more than at our old school. And you make friends easily."

"I'm not worried about school," Caroline said. "I'm looking forward to *that*!"

As Ashleigh slid into bed that night, after carefully piling her horse magazines on the floor, she thought about school the next day. Unlike Caroline, she wasn't looking forward to it all. In fact, she was scared. All those new kids to meet—and a new schedule and new teachers! Ashleigh didn't hate school, but they didn't study things she was interested in, like horse care. Biology was okay, and English, because she loved to read. But math, as far as she was concerned, was a waste of time, and so was history. The only history that had ever interested her was the history of horses and Thoroughbred bloodlines.

She turned over on her side. What would the new school be like? It was probably a lot bigger than her old school. Would she remember her locker combination? That always scared her, because she'd had trouble with one when she first went into middle school. Her locker wouldn't open, and she was late to class three days in a row. She'd ended up carrying all of her books around all day. At least at her old school she'd been friends with most of the kids. She and her best friend, Mona, had spent almost all their free time to-gether. They'd known each other since kindergarten, and liked all the same things. She'd already started a letter to Mona, telling her about her first day at Town-send Acres. Here she wouldn't know anyone.

She turned over again. Caroline was asleep. Typi-cally, she had carefully laid out the outfit she was go-ing to wear the next day, after about an hour of pick-ing and choosing. The only time Caroline had seemed happy that night was while she was trying on clothes. In the morning Ashleigh would dig her own clothes out of the still-unpacked boxes on the floor.

Ashleigh stared out at the night sky. She heard the muffled whinny of a horse who wasn't settled for the night either. Ashleigh still missed Edgardale so much, but she thought of her day and all the things she'd done, and of Holly and April. Finally Ashleigh closed her eyes and drifted off to sleep.

2

"AREN'T YOU NERVOUS AT *ALL*?" ASHLEIGH ASKED CAROLINE AS they waited at the end of the drive for the bus.

Caroline straightened the bottom of her sweater for about the seventeenth time. "Well, maybe a little— this school is so much bigger than our old one."

That was exactly what Ashleigh was afraid of. She played with her backpack, swinging it around by its shoulder straps. As usual, she was dressed in jeans and a cotton shirt, with her dark hair pulled back into a short ponytail. "I'd rather stay here."

Caroline gave her sister a look of amazement. "So you could clean out stalls, and all that disgusting stuff?"

"It's not disgusting—" Ashleigh didn't get a chance to finish. The bus drew around the corner and stopped in front of them. She let Caroline get on first. As Ashleigh climbed the steps and looked down the aisle, she saw a sea of strange faces. The bus was almost full, but Caroline found an empty seat halfway back and slid into it. Ashleigh sat next to her.

The girl in the seat in front of them turned around. She had a mass of shoulder-length curly blond hair and looked about Ashleigh's age. She smiled at them. "Did you guys just move to Townsend Acres?"

Both girls nodded, but Caroline was the first to speak. "Our parents are managing the breeding farm. I'm Caroline Griffen, and this is my sister, Ashleigh."

"Hi. I'm Linda March. We have a place about a mile up the road. You like Townsend Acres?"

Caroline shrugged, but Ashleigh answered. "It's so big. I haven't gotten used to it yet."

"I saw their stables once—they're fantastic. My father's a trainer, but we only board horses for other people. We just have a few exercise horses of our own."

"You like horses, then?" Ashleigh asked.

"I love them!" Linda exclaimed. "My father's teaching me to train."

"He is? Do you ride?"

"Sure. I ride the exercise horses all the time. Do you ride?"

Ashleigh nodded. "My parents are going to find me a horse on the farm that I can use."

Caroline yawned. "You must be in middle school," she said to Linda.

22

"Sixth grade."

"So am I," Ashleigh said. "Maybe I'll be in some of your classes."

"Do you have your schedule yet?" Linda asked.

"No, I have to pick it up in the office."

"I'll go with you," Linda offered. "Then I can show you around a little."

This was better than Ashleigh had hoped—meeting a new friend on the bus, and one who loved horses! She glanced over at Caroline to see what she thought, but her sister was very carefully looking around the bus, checking out the other kids.

When the bus dropped them off in front of the school complex, Caroline gave Ashleigh a careless wave and headed toward the high school building. "See you tonight," she said.

Linda quickly pulled Ashleigh off toward the middle school entrance. "You'll like it here," she said. "The teachers aren't too bad, and you can meet some of my friends."

She led Ashleigh around a turn in the hall and into the office, and presented her to the school secretary, Mrs. Wislow.

The secretary smiled at Ashleigh. "Welcome to Henry Clay, Ashleigh. We've been expecting you. I have your schedule." She passed it over the counter. "And here's your locker number, combination, and some information about the school. I see you and

23

Linda have already become friends. Maybe she can help you find your bearings."

"Sure," Linda said.

"And stop by the office if you have any questions at all," Mrs. Wislow added.

"Thank you," Ashleigh answered. The two girls studied Ashleigh's schedule. "All right!" Linda said. "We have the same homeroom, and we're in English and science together. Come on, let's go find your locker."

By the end of the day, Ashleigh had decided Henry Clay wasn't such a bad school. Her teachers seemed nice enough, and none of them expected her to do much on her first day—except for Mr. Jordan in math, who talked too fast and frowned a lot. At lunch she met two of Linda's friends, Corey and Jennifer. The girls started talking a mile a minute as soon as they sat down. Ashleigh didn't know the people or places they were talking about, and she couldn't have gotten a word in anyway. She ate her sandwich in silence and was feeling a little dizzy by the time the two girls finished their lunches and rushed off.

Linda turned to Ashleigh and grinned. "Yeah, I know, they talk a lot, but they're pretty nice, and they like horses. They come over and ride with me sometimes. Plus, Corey's the best player on the sixth-grade tennis team."

Linda was on the tennis team, too, and was staying

after school for tennis practice. Ashleigh said good-bye to her after their last class, then headed for her bus. She saved a seat for her sister, but Caroline was so late coming from the high school that she almost missed the bus.

"What took you so long?" Ashleigh asked as Caro sat down next to her.

Caroline was breathless but beaming. "I was talking to some friends I met—they live right outside Lexington and asked me to come to the mall and go shopping with them tomorrow. I can't wait!"

Ashleigh didn't mind getting new clothes, but she hated hanging around in stores and trying things on. She didn't understand how Caroline could think it was fun.

"I still have some money saved from my birthday," Caroline said excitedly. "I hope Mom says it's all right. Marcy said I can have supper at their house, and she'll drive me home—she just got her license!"

It was good to see Caroline smiling. Ashleigh listened with half an ear as her sister bubbled on about her classes and the other kids she'd met. The rest of Ashleigh's concentration was on the scenery beyond the window—the green paddocks where Thorough-breds ran free. She thought about her first day at Henry Clay and how glad she was that she'd met Linda. But everything still seemed so new and kind of scary. She only snapped to when her sister jabbed her in the ribs with her elbow. "Ashleigh! We're here!"

Ashleigh quickly gathered up her backpack, now filled with books, and hurried after her sister. As they started up the drive, they passed the main turning to Clay Townsend's huge house at the top of the rise, then followed the left fork to their own house and the stables. Several of the grazing horses lifted their heads to gaze at them curiously.

"What are you going to do this afternoon?" Caroline asked.

Ashleigh shrugged. "I don't know. I guess I'll go out to the barns."

"After I ask Mom about going with Marcy tomorrow," Caroline said cheerfully, "I'm going to finish fixing up my side of the room. Why don't you put your stuff away? You haven't unpacked anything yet."

Ashleigh toyed with a strand of hair that had slipped loose from her ponytail. "I will sometime. I don't feel like it this afternoon. It doesn't really feel like home yet anyway."

The stable yard was busier than it had been on Sunday. Several cars and pickup trucks were parked in the parking area near the barns. Caroline went straight out to their parents' office, and Ashleigh went into the house, then up the stairs to their bedroom. She flung her backpack on her bed and changed into her everyday jeans. She was coming back down the stairs when her sister hurried into the house, grinning. "Mom said it's okay! I've got to call Marcy!" Caroline breezed past in the direction of the phone.

Ashleigh gave her sister a puzzled frown. How could Caroline adjust to their new home so quickly—especially when she'd been so miserable the night before?

Jesse and April waved hello as Ashleigh stepped into the foaling barn. They had news for her, too. "Three Foot dropped her foal this morning." April leaned her pitchfork against the side of the stall she was cleaning. "A beautiful little colt. Want to see?"

Ashleigh wasn't sure if she did. The sight of a newborn foal would make her think of the foal that had died at Edgardale. Yet deep inside she was curious, and couldn't resist. She followed April down to the end of the barn. Together they looked over the stall door at the mare, who was proudly nuzzling her copper-colored foal. The foal looked strong for a newborn, and he was perfectly formed.

"Townsend Pride's?" Ashleigh asked, appreciating his beauty.

"Looks just like his dad, doesn't he?" April said. "Mr. Townsend'll be happy. He's been looking forward to this foal."

Ashleigh's father walked up from the other end of the barn. "Hello there!" he called. "Nice-looking foal, isn't he? How was your first day at school?"

27

"Oh, okay," Ashleigh said.

"Just okay?" he sympathized. "Well, the first day's always the hardest. It'll get better. Bill had to go into Lexington. Your mother's busy in the office, and I want to go check on a couple of the mares. I know Jesse and April will need some help getting the stalls ready, if you feel like it."

Ashleigh decided she'd rather be busy than just hang around. And she liked April. "Sure," she said. "I guess I can."

For the next hour Ashleigh helped pitchfork dirty bedding into a wheelbarrow and take it outside. Then she helped fill the water buckets and hay nets. The work was so familiar to Ashleigh. She slipped into the rhythm, and for a while forgot she wasn't at Edgardale but at Townsend Acres.

Each of the mares had an individual feeding schedule, and April and Jesse checked their charts before measuring out grain and vitamin supplements. When all thirty stalls were immaculate and the center aisle of the barn had been swept and hosed down, April and Jesse had a couple of free hours to themselves before they brought in the mares and foals for the night.

"Thanks a lot for helping," April said as the three of them put the pitchforks, wheelbarrows, and buckets away in the storage room.

"That's okay," Ashleigh answered with a smile. "I've mucked out a lot of stalls before this."

"Holly's in the small paddock by herself," April added. "Maybe you want to go out and say hello."

"She's alone?" Ashleigh asked, surprised. The mares who hadn't foaled were usually put out in a huge paddock together.

"I think your dad's worried about her."

Ashleigh frowned. "Is she sick?"

"No, just old. He doesn't want any of the younger mares pushing her around."

"They can't push that old lady around," Jesse commented. "She knows how to hold her own. But your father's right to keep her quiet. Bill's been worried about her, too. Oh, she'll be okay," he added quickly when he saw Ashleigh's frightened expression. "We'll just give her a little extra TLC."

"You're sure?" Ashleigh asked anxiously. Just the mention of a sick horse brought back all the horrible memories of her last days at Edgardale.

"Positive," Jesse and April said in one breath.

But Ashleigh felt uncertain as she walked outside and leaned against the paddock fence. Maybe it would be better if she didn't get close to any horse—ever again.

Holly lifted her head and perked her ears when she saw Ashleigh, and trotted right to the fence. She nickered happily to Ashleigh. Despite herself, Ashleigh felt her heart melt at the mare's warm greeting.

"Hi, girl," she said, rubbing her hand along Holly's

neck as the mare leaned her head over the railing. "So you remember me, huh? I'll bet you're looking for a carrot." Ashleigh reached in her pocket. Out of habit, she had taken a couple from the supply of treats in the feed room. Holly gently took the carrot, then bobbed her head against Ashleigh's shoulder in thanks.

Ashleigh felt her eyes grow hot with tears. This was just like being with Stardust. Stardust would have given her the same greeting, and the two horses really did look so much alike. Holly was a little taller and had more elegant lines than Stardust, who wasn't a Thoroughbred, but their coloring was identical, and they both had the same soft expression in their brown eyes. "You're a good old girl, aren't you?" Ashleigh said in a choked voice.

Holly gazed at her through long lashes and touched her velvety nose to Ashleigh's hand. One of the other mares in the big neighboring paddock whinnied loudly. Holly suddenly lifted her head and answered back with a whinny of her own.

"You're lonesome in here all by yourself, aren't you?" Ashleigh sympathized. Holly whoofed gently, then lowered her head and nibbled at the lush grass near the paddock fence. Ashleigh climbed up and sat on the paddock rail. "I've been feeling pretty lonesome, too. I miss our old place and my friends . . . and my old horse. I hated coming here."

Holly looked up.

"You understand, don't you?" Ashleigh sighed. "Stardust would have understood, too. I hope she's all right. The new people who bought our farm promised they'd take good care of her, but I know she's going to miss me. She's not going to know why I went away."

Holly touched her nose to Ashleigh's leg, and Ashleigh laid a hand on the mare's head. Under Holly's gentle gaze, Ashleigh felt herself relaxing. For the first time since she'd arrived at Townsend Acres, she felt a trace of the happiness she used to feel when she was with Stardust. The air smelled of fresh grass, and the spring sunshine was warm on her head and shoulders.

Ashleigh looked out at the rolling green pastures surrounding her. She thought of the wonderful rides she'd had on Stardust. What fun they could have had here! Townsend Acres was so much bigger, with so many more places to go. But Stardust wasn't here. Ashleigh sighed miserably, but as she watched the grazing Thoroughbreds, she couldn't help wondering what it would be like to ride one of *them* out over the rolling hills instead. She thought of Brad Townsend and how well he'd ridden his colt. She didn't like Brad, but she knew a good rider when she saw one.

Without realizing what she was doing, Ashleigh straddled the paddock rail and leaned forward in a jockey's crouch, picturing herself galloping around the training oval. She was a good rider. Her parents had taught all of their children to ride almost as soon as they could walk, but riding a Thoroughbred racehorse was different—much more demanding and dangerous. Ashleigh knew that all Thoroughbreds were descended from three famous stallions imported to England in the 1700s—the Darley Arabian, the Byerly Turk, and the Godolphin Arabian. They were bred for speed and could be headstrong, too, and they would be much harder to handle than easygoing Stardust. What a challenge and thrill it would be to ride in the saddle of a horse like that!

"What do you think, Holly?" she asked. "April told me that you used to race. She said you were really good."

The mare looked up and tossed her head. "I know, you're too old now, but maybe when your foal is big enough . . ." Ashleigh stopped herself. She hadn't really thought much about Holly's foal until then. She wasn't sure she wanted to think about it—in case something went wrong.

She'd lost all track of time and was surprised when her mother walked over. "So here you are! It's time to bring the mares in, and I've got to go start dinner. You must have some homework to do, too."

"Only a little."

Her mother leaned her arms on the rail and studied Holly. "I can guess why you're out here. She reminds you of old Stardust, doesn't she?"

Ashleigh nodded. "Yes. A lot."

"We all miss the horses. It's not going to be easy." Her mother paused, still watching Holly. "I have an idea, Ashleigh. You know that April and Jesse are both pretty busy."

"Mmm. They were glad I helped them today."

"How would you like to take over as Holly's groom?"

Ashleigh stared at her mother in surprise. "Me? I-I don't know . . ."

"I think you could handle Holly. She's quiet and gentle and it would be good for you to be busy. You've always loved working in the barn with the horses."

"Yes, but—" Ashleigh hesitated, biting her lip.

"You're afraid of getting too attached again, aren't you?" her mother said.

"Yes," Ashleigh whispered.

"I know how you feel, but you can't close yourself off just because you're afraid of getting hurt. None of us will ever forget, but I think we'll all recover from losing Edgardale faster if we start getting involved here. What do you say? Why not try it for a few days and see?"

"But Dad's worried about Holly."

"Only normal worry. He worries about all the mares. Holly's just a little older than the others, but she's fit. She'll be fine."

Still Ashleigh hesitated. She was afraid. She

couldn't help it. If anything should happen to Holly or her foal—

Then Holly lifted her head and walked slowly up to Ashleigh. The mare gave her a soft look.

Ashleigh felt her heart melt all over again. "You want me to be your groom?" she asked.

The old mare nickered, and nudged Ashleigh again. Of course, she didn't really understand, but she seemed to. Ashleigh considered. She felt so uncertain, but maybe her mother was right, and she should get more involved. "Okay," she finally said. "I'll try."

Her mother smiled. "Good. Run in and get a lead shank and bring her inside."

Ashleigh slid down from the rail. But as she entered the barn, she slowed her steps reluctantly. Was she ready to do this? She found her father checking over each of the mares as Jesse and April brought them in. She told him what her mother had suggested. She almost hoped he'd say no, but he nodded. "That'd be a big help! We could sure use an extra hand right now. April can go out with you today, just to make sure there's no problem. You know where to find the shanks."

As the two girls walked out to Holly's paddock, Ashleigh had a sinking feeling in her stomach. But it was too late to change her mind now.

April watched as Ashleigh entered the paddock and clipped the lead shank to Holly's halter. The mare followed calmly. She knew her warm stall and evening meal would be waiting. As they entered the barn, Holly lifted her head and answered the calls of the mares already in their stalls.

"I've filled her feed bucket," April said, "and the brushes are right outside here in her box. Just go over her lightly. Doesn't look like she's been rolling in the mud."

While Holly contentedly chewed her oats, Ashleigh gently brushed the old mare's reddish coat. Holly rippled her muscles with pleasure and gave a few quiet grunts. "You like that, don't you?" Ashleigh smiled. She brushed out the mare's long mane and tail, then used a hoof-pick to get the dirt out of the mare's feet.

As she worked, she remembered all the times she'd groomed Stardust. The feel of the brush in her hand was so familiar—as were the smells of horse and hay and the sounds of Holly crunching on her grain. Everything was so peaceful. For a moment she felt like she was back with Stardust at Edgardale before everything had gone so wrong. She found herself thinking again of Holly's foal. It should be born soon. By late April most of the other mares had given birth. Holly was one of the last left. The foal would be a spindly bundle of legs at first, but if all went well, it would grow tall and strong and graceful. It would probably have the same copper coloring as Holly and its father, Townsend Pride.

Before leaving Holly's stall, Ashleigh double-checked Holly's water bucket and hay net, then she laid her cheek against the mare's neck. "I'll see you tomorrow morning. Rest well tonight."

Holly nickered softly and went back to her feed. Ashleigh slipped out of the stall, carefully latched the door behind her, and took one last look at the mare.

3

ASHLEIGH WOKE UP AT FIVE. WHEN SHE SAW THE DIM DAWN light seeping through the window, she thought for a moment she was still at Edgardale. Then she remembered where she was. She remembered, too, that she now had Holly to groom, and she threw her legs over the side of the bed.

She dressed quickly and quietly, careful not to wake her sleeping sister, then hurried downstairs and out to the foaling barn.

April and Jesse looked up and waved as Ashleigh passed them outside the barn. Ashleigh's parents were already in the stable office, sipping coffee and looking over the day's schedule. Their day would be full, Ashleigh knew. First they'd check over all the mares and foals before the horses were led outside, then they'd look over the feed charts and inoculation records for each animal, and of course, there was always the possibility of a new foal being born. The mares who'd already foaled were being bred again, and her parents would arrange for those mares to be brought over to the breeding barns. There weren't too many quiet moments in a breeding stable during the spring.

Ashleigh didn't stop, but went straight to Holly's stall. The mare was obviously glad to see her. She thrust her head over the stall door and nickered a welcome. As Ashleigh stopped at the stall, Holly affectionately nudged her.

Suddenly Ashleigh felt a little more cheerful. "Hungry, aren't you?" She smiled, rubbing Holly's ears. "I'll go get your breakfast."

In the feed room Ashleigh followed the chart on the wall and carefully portioned out Holly's morning meal of grain. She brought it back to the stall, and as the mare dug in, Ashleigh collected Holly's brushes and started grooming. From time to time Holly glanced back over shoulder, watching Ashleigh work. Soon Ashleigh began humming softly to herself, forgetting her worries and enjoying the quiet companionship of the mare.

By the time Ashleigh was finished, Holly's coat was shining like silk. The mare seemed happy with the result and nickered her approval. Ashleigh grinned. "So you like the way I groom you, huh?"

April and Jesse were beginning to lead some of the mares and foals outside to the paddocks. The horses were full of energy after their night in the barn. The mares' shod hooves clattered on the concrete floor as they pranced and strained on their leads in anticipation of going outdoors. Their foals frolicked along beside them.

Ashleigh clipped the lead shank to Holly's halter, opened the stall door, and led the mare down the barn aisle and outside. Gentle rays of morning sunshine slanted through the trees and over the green countryside. Holly shook her head and whinnied in excitement. Once inside her paddock, the mare gave Ashleigh a parting nicker, then she trotted off heavily over the springy grass. Ashleigh watched until Holly settled down to graze, then she returned to the barn to muck out Holly's stall.

Ashleigh pitchforked the dirty bedding into a wheelbarrow to be taken outside. She breathed in the smells of hay and horses and leather and realized how much she liked the physical effort and the atmosphere of the stables. She'd just finished adding fresh bedding to Holly's stall when April strolled over.

"We're pretty well caught up this morning," she told Ashleigh. "Why don't you go over and watch the training for a while?"

"I hadn't thought of that," Ashleigh said, checking her watch. She had enjoyed watching the horses work their first day at Townsend Acres. And at least the training didn't bring any reminders of Edgardale. "I guess I do have time before school," she added. "Maybe I will. Thanks, April."

Ashleigh made a last inspection of Holly's stall, then set off up the drive. In the early morning light, the pastures were a misty green. The air smelled crisp and fresh and echoed with birdcalls and neighing horses. It could be nice here, she decided—if only she didn't miss Edgardale so much!

The training area was busy. Stable hands were walking and rubbing down the horses that had already been exercised. Grooms were leading other saddled horses from the stable. Exercise riders moved in a steady stream to and from the track.

Ashleigh tried not to get in anyone's way. She found a spot under the trees with a good view of the track and settled down to watch.

Three horses were out on the oval. Ken Maddock was standing near the rail, stopwatch in hand. He squinted in concentration as the horses breezed past. Ashleigh watched the galloping Thoroughbreds in awe. The horses' feet barely seemed to touch the ground as they sped around the track. Some riders finished their gallops, walked out of the ring, and paused to talk to Mr. Maddock. Other riders rode onto the track.

One of them was a girl. Ashleigh only knew she was a girl because of the long blond braid that hung down from under her hat. She was on a big bay, and the

40

horse was acting up—bucking, prancing—but the girl sat quietly in the saddle. From the way the horse's ears flicked back, Ashleigh guessed the girl was talking to her mount. *She's doing what I'd do,* Ashleigh thought. Gradually the big horse calmed down, and in a moment horse and rider were moving off smoothly around the track in a warm-up jog.

A little while later, Ashleigh spotted Brad Townsend on his colt, approaching the oval. Brad's colt was in high spirits, too, and Brad was obviously having trouble getting him to calm down and concentrate. The colt began to rear. Brad jerked on the colt's reins and smacked him with his whip.

Suddenly Ashleigh heard a grumbling voice beside her. "That's not the way to handle him! You'll ruin him!"

She spun to her right and saw Charlie Burke standing several yards away. He was glaring at the boy and the colt. She glanced back to the track. Mr. Maddock was calling something to Brad, and finally Brad got his colt under control.

The colt was beautiful, and he moved like the wind when Brad urged him from a jog into a gallop. Ashleigh couldn't take her eyes off them, although she thought about what the old trainer had said.

She was so engrossed that she jumped when Charlie Burke brushed past her, scowling. He slammed his floppy hat down on his head and barely seemed to notice her as he stalked off toward the barn.

Brad had finished his gallop and was talking with Mr. Maddock. His colt's body, heated after all the exercise, steamed in the crisp morning air.

Ashleigh glanced at her watch and gave a little gasp. She'd never get home in time to change and get to the school bus if she didn't leave now. She raced away from the ring and arrived at the house just in time to change and gulp down a bowl of cereal before rushing to the bus with Caroline.

On Friday Ashleigh doodled in her notebook during last-period history class and thought about her first week in school. She'd met some kids and had signed up for chorus, since she liked singing and practice was during school, not after. She and Linda were becoming close friends. She felt as if they'd known each other for ages, not just a few days. And there was Holly. Even though Ashleigh had been afraid at first, she was growing closer and closer to the old mare. It was almost like having Stardust back again. With every passing day, Ashleigh found herself getting more involved in her life at Townsend Acres—liking it just a little bit more and feeling a few less pangs of homesickness for Edgardale.

The classroom window was open and a warm breeze drifted in. Ashleigh wanted to be out there, not stuck inside. Her father said Holly would probably foal within the next few days. The mare was big and heavy, and the last couple of days she'd seemed tired. Ashleigh was getting worried.

"Ashleigh, maybe you can answer that question for us."

Ashleigh started and looked up guiltily at her teacher. "I'm sorry, Miss Vost, could you repeat the question?"

Miss Vost tried to hide her smile. "I know, you'd all rather be out of here, but remember, you have a test coming up next week. We were talking about the League of Nations. In what year did President Wilson's commission draft its Covenant?"

Ashleigh didn't have a clue. She thought furiously. *League of Nations . . . that was right after World War I, wasn't it?* She took a wild guess. "1919?"

"Right."

Ashleigh was amazed, and Miss Vost looked like she knew it was a lucky guess, but she directed her next question to Danny McCarthy, who was slouching down in his seat with his eyes half closed.

Finally the bell rang. Ashleigh gathered up her books and rushed out the door to her locker. She quickly selected some books, called good-bye to a few kids she knew, and hurried to her bus.

Linda was waiting and had saved Ashleigh a seat.

Caroline was sitting at the back of the bus with some new friends she'd made.

"I'm so excited!" Linda cried as Ashleigh sat down. "Dad's taking me to Churchill Downs over the weekend. He's bringing three of the horses he's trained. He told me I could help groom."

"There must be so much going on at the track!" Ashleigh sighed, envying Linda. "All those gorgeous horses. I've never been to Churchill Downs. You'll have to tell me all about it when you get back."

"It'll be really exciting, since it's Kentucky Derby weekend."

"And to have your own horse racing!" Ashleigh exclaimed.

"Well, we don't have any racing in the Derby. And the horses aren't really ours—Dad just trains them," Linda said.

"I know, but it's almost the same. Mr. Townsend will be there with Townsend Victor. Everyone thinks he's going to win." The bus was pulling up at Townsend Acres, and Ashleigh jumped up from her seat. "Tell me *everything* when you get back!"

"I will! I'll even take notes! See you Monday."

Ashleigh ran up the drive, planning to see how Holly was doing. But when she looked over to the mare's paddock, she saw it was empty. That could only mean one thing—Holly was having her foal!

4

IT TOOK A MOMENT FOR ASHLEIGH'S EYES TO ADJUST TO THE darker interior of the foaling barn. When they did, she saw her mother and father, Bill Parks, and Dr. James, the vet, gathered in and around Holly's stall. April and Jesse had stopped work, too, and were watching anxiously. None of them looked very happy.

Ashleigh heard the vet mutter to her father, "A shame . . . one of Townsend Pride's foals . . . and this mare's had her last. Townsend will be disappointed. But you've got that other colt. He's doing nicely."

Ashleigh's stomach clenched. "What's wrong?" she asked softly as she reached the stall.

"Holly's just had her foal," her mother said quietly. "A filly."

But the tone of her mother's voice frightened Ashleigh. She stepped into the stall. Holly was standing at

45

the rear. On the thick bedding near her feet lay a long-legged foal—a very small foal. Her still-damp coat was the color of copper, but she had four white stockings and a snip of white at the end of her nose. She looked at Ashleigh with huge, dark eyes too big for her finely tapered face. The appealing look went straight to Ashleigh's heart. "She's beautiful," Ashleigh whispered.

"Sweetheart," her father said gently. "I don't think this little filly's going to make it."

"What do you mean? She seems awfully small, but—"

"It was a difficult delivery. Because of Holly's age, she had a hard time of it. The foal's weak . . . very weak. She didn't breathe on her own at first. Dr. James had to resuscitate her. She still hasn't made any effort to stand. That's not a good sign."

"Can't you help her?" Ashleigh said in a small voice.

Her mother laid a hand on her shoulder. "Hold on, Ashleigh."

"It's better to leave them alone for a while," the vet said. "Too much human contact isn't good at this stage. The mare and filly have to bond. If the foal survives, that bond is essential." As he spoke, Holly lowered her head and gently licked her foal. She nickered softly and nudged the tiny body with her nose. The foal remained curled up on the bedding and made no effort to move. Holly tried again without success.

Ashleigh looked from her father to the vet to Bill Parks. Their faces registered the same sad resignation. All Ashleigh could think of were the horses lost at Edgardale. She wanted to cry. She couldn't stand to see another horse die—especially this foal—Holly's foal—the foal she'd been waiting for.

Her mother saw Ashleigh's expression. "We haven't given up yet," she said quickly. "Some foals are slow to stand. Let's just wait awhile and see." But Mrs. Griffen didn't sound very hopeful, and her face was drawn and pale. "Maybe you should go up to the house."

Ashleigh shook her head. She couldn't leave! There must be something she could do.

But as the minutes ticked slowly past, Ashleigh felt the fear of uncertainty. She gripped her hands together so tightly that her knuckles turned white, but she didn't notice. Ashleigh thought her heart was going to break as she watched Holly licking and nuzzling her foal. It took all her willpower not to go in and help the mare. Holly was so gentle, so loving, coaxing her foal with whoofing breaths. "Please try to stand up," Ashleigh whispered. But the foal didn't. She lay helplessly on the bedding, looking more dead than alive. Only her huge eyes held a spark.

"We've got to do something!" Ashleigh finally cried. "Even if she won't stand on her own, can't we feed her?" She looked at each of the adults with pleading eyes. Her parents' faces showed their own pain and worry. They were thinking of Edgardale, too.

Dr. James answered Ashleigh. "She needs her mother's first milk," he said. "The colostrum contains important antibodies to prevent disease."

"I could hold her while she nursed. . . ."

"You could try," the vet answered. "Though I'm afraid she may refuse to nurse. A foal this weak will need constant care. If she does make it, she'll be slow developing. It's not likely she'll ever be a successful racer or a very valuable broodmare either. I seriously doubt Clay Townsend would consider the care worth it. He hasn't got the extra staff, and he'd consider the added expense a bad business decision."

"No!" Ashleigh said. "You can't just let her die. If no one else wants to save her, I'll take care of her! Mr. Townsend doesn't have to pay *me.* Holly and I can do it, can't we, girl?"

Before any of the adults could stop her, Ashleigh walked over to the foal and knelt down beside her. Holly nickered, showing her trust in her friend. Ashleigh rubbed a hand over the filly's damp copper coat. The foal looked at her with big, brown eyes. "You're going to be okay," Ashleigh said gently. "I'm going to help you stand up. You've got to stand up and nurse, or you'll never be strong."

Holly leaned her head down to her foal again. "I know, Holly," Ashleigh said. "You don't want her to die either." Ashleigh gently stroked the foal's side. How soft and warm she felt, but so fragile, too. Ashleigh could feel each of her little ribs under the fuzzy coat. "Please try," Ashleigh whispered to the foal. "Your mother wants you to try, too."

The foal flicked her ears toward Ashleigh. She seemed to understand. She made a feeble effort to move her legs. It hurt terribly to watch her struggle— and she didn't have the strength to get them beneath her. She quickly collapsed down into the bedding.

"You can do it," Ashleigh said, her throat choking up.

"Ashleigh," her father and mother said in one breath. "Don't. If she's that weak, you can't save her."

"You'll only make it worse for yourself," her mother added. "We know how you feel. We feel the same, but sometimes it's beyond human power to save an animal."

"We can't let another horse die!"

"We didn't *let* our other horses die—we tried everything we could!"

"I'm not giving up!" Ashleigh thrust her arms under the filly's body and lifted, holding the weight of the foal in her arms. "Come on," she pleaded with the filly. The baby horse felt like a cuddly bundle, but as delicate as a china doll. "Stand up. Please! Get your legs underneath you. You're Holly's foal. You have to make it!"

As Ashleigh held the foal's midsection, the filly weakly kicked out her legs. Ashleigh lifted her higher in the air until the long legs straightened. Gently she set the filly down. But the tiny horse didn't have the strength. Her legs immediately began to wobble and fold. Ashleigh tightened her grip and kept the foal from falling, then she carried her to Holly's side. "You've got to eat," she said.

Holly swung her head around to the foal and nickered encouragement. As frail as she was, the little filly instinctively knew what she should do. Ashleigh gently directed the little head toward Holly's teat. At first the foal did nothing. Ashleigh coaxed her, "Please try. You'll die otherwise. I can't let you." Finally, after tasting a few drops of milk, the foal began to nurse.

Ashleigh gently laid her cheek on the foal's short back. "I knew you could do it." She sighed. "I knew it."

Dr. James spoke from behind her. "I don't want to discourage you, but getting her to nurse isn't the single solution. The difficult birth may have caused other problems. I won't know for sure until I get the tests back. She's so weak, she's going to be much more susceptible to disease. I'd give her only a fifty-fifty chance of survival."

"I don't care," Ashleigh said. "I'm still going to try."

The vet sighed. "You're a fighter—I'll say that for

you. Of course, the decision's not up to me—it's up to your parents and Mr. Townsend."

Ashleigh turned anxiously to her father and mother. They both looked uneasy and troubled.

"Ashleigh, we want to save her, too," her mother said. "But I don't want to see you hurt again. No matter what you do, she might not make it. Wouldn't it be better to keep a distance . . . let Bill or your father—"

"No," Ashleigh said. She knew what her mother was suggesting. "Please! I'd feel worse if I didn't . . . even if she doesn't . . ." Ashleigh couldn't finish. She had to bite her lip to keep from crying. She hugged the little foal closer.

"What do you think?" Mrs. Griffen said to Mr. Griffen.

He rubbed a hand over his face. "Obviously, it's against everything I believe in to give up without a fight. Townsend may feel otherwise, but since he's away for a few days, I'll have to go with my own gut feeling. I want to try to save the foal, and the staff have their hands full this time of year." He looked at Ashleigh, then nodded. "She can give it a shot."

Ashleigh let out a shuddering breath.

Dr. James picked up his bag from the floor. "I hope you're not making a mistake," he said. "I don't know what Townsend will say. Derek, I'll let you know the results of the blood tests. I'll be by the first of the week and check over all the foals. Call if you need me before." He glanced meaningfully at the foal and left the stall.

Bill motioned to April and Jesse. "Okay, you two, back to work." But before he left, he patted Ashleigh's shoulder. "I'll be rooting for you. You let me know if you need help."

"Thanks," Ashleigh said gratefully.

When Bill and the grooms were gone, Ashleigh's mother knelt down beside her. "Are you sure about this? The vet's right. Her chances aren't good. You know from what happened at Edgardale that animals sometimes die no matter what you try to do to save them. If you get too attached to this filly, it's going to hurt all the more if the worst happens."

"I don't care, Mom. I *have* to try and save her."

Her mother leaned over and kissed Ashleigh's cheek. "Okay. Go for it, then."

"We'll give you a hand whenever we can," her father added, "though you know we're all going to be pretty busy until the last of the foals is born."

"I know. But I'll be all right," Ashleigh said. "I can do it." The filly had finished nursing, and Ashleigh carefully carried her a few feet away and nestled her back on the bedding. The foal curled her legs beneath her and lowered her head onto Ashleigh's lap. The effort of nursing had exhausted her. Ashleigh's heart sank, but she didn't let her parents see it.

"Let her rest," her father said. "We'll stop by later."

Ashleigh stroked the foal. "Don't worry, you're going to be fine," she whispered, trying to reassure herself, too. "You can rest for now, and later I'll help you up again. You need to get strong as fast as you can." Yet as she looked down at the frail little horse, she was afraid. Would this beautiful animal live to run around the paddock like the other foals? Would Ashleigh lose another horse she loved? She knew how badly it would hurt. But she had to fight for this foal's life. She looked down at the copper bundle curled up near her lap. The filly's finely shaped head with its oversized ears wasn't even as long as Ashleigh's thigh. Her still-soft hooves would have fit easily into Ashleigh's cupped palm, but already Ashleigh could see the potential of beauty and grace—an awkward miniature of the foal's father, Townsend Pride.

Holly came to stand beside them and dropped her head. She nuzzled Ashleigh's hair, then leaned down to nuzzle her foal. "She's going to grow up to be just like you, Holly," Ashleigh said quietly. "She'll be just as sweet, and a wonderful racehorse, too." She rubbed the mare's velvety nose. "We'll save her, girl, don't worry." If only Ashleigh could feel so sure.

In a little while, when the foal seemed rested, Ashleigh gently lifted her to her feet again and brought her to Holly's side to nurse. When she was finished, Ashleigh and the foal cuddled back down in the stall.

April and Jesse came by and brought fresh water and feed for Holly. "How's she doing?" April asked.

"Great," Ashleigh said fiercely. In all honesty, the foal wasn't any better, but Ashleigh wasn't going to admit it.

"Maybe," Jesse said skeptically. "Lucky she's got you around, anyway. Nobody else could spend that much time with her. There're too many other horses to take care of and plenty of healthy foals. They always figure they'll lose one or two, and a foal that's weak to start with . . ." He shrugged.

April glared at him. "You don't have to sound so heartless!"

"Facts of life," he said.

"Don't pay any attention to him, Ashleigh. He likes to talk tough, but he's really a marshmallow underneath. He'll be around checking the foal whenever you're not here."

Jesse was embarrassed by April's description and stomped off. "April," he called over his shoulder, "you've got horses to bring in."

"Mine'll be in before yours," she called back. "I'll see you later," she said to Ashleigh, giving her a thumbs-up sign.

5

ASHLEIGH DIDN'T LEAVE THE FOAL'S SIDE ONCE DURING THE night. Since there was no school the next day, her parents didn't mind. They came by every hour during the evening to see how she was doing, and her mother brought her a sandwich for dinner and a warm blanket. The foal seemed a little more alert. She lifted her head and looked around, but she still made no attempt to rise on her own.

Before Mr. and Mrs. Griffen went in to bed, they stopped by the stall one last time. Her father carefully looked the foal over. "We'll just have to wait and see," he said. "I'll be down first thing in the morning. Try to get a little rest, sweetheart. If you need us in a hurry, call from the office phone."

But Ashleigh couldn't rest. If she fell asleep, something might happen to Holly's foal. Ashleigh cradled her and talked to her. Again and again she carried her

55

over to Holly to nurse, then held the foal close on the bedding while she rested. The little animal never balked. She gazed at Ashleigh with her big, trusting eyes and snuggled closer to her human friend. Ashleigh's feeling for the filly deepened with each passing hour, and she knew just how devastated she'd be if the filly didn't survive.

Ashleigh was close to exhaustion when her father came by early the next morning. But she had to report that the foal had still made no effort to stand on her own.

"You need some sleep," her father said. "I can stay with her a few hours, and Bill can check on her."

"I can't leave her, Dad. She'll think I'm deserting her."

"No, she won't. I'll stay right with her. At least go up and get some breakfast."

"I'm not hungry."

"That's an order. You can't go without food."

Reluctantly Ashleigh rose. Her father quickly took her place, but as Ashleigh started to leave the stall, the foal lifted her head and stared after her. Ashleigh stopped in her tracks. Her father motioned her on. "I'll be right here till you get back."

Ashleigh raced up to the house. Her mother was just leaving the kitchen for the barn and gave Ashleigh a startled, worried look. "Is she all right?"

"Yes. Dad's staying with her. He told me to come have breakfast."

"I was just going to tell you the same thing." Her mother turned in the doorway and went back into the kitchen. "I made you something hot. Here, sit down." She reached in the oven, took out a covered plate of scrambled eggs and bacon, and slid it in front of Ashleigh. She sat in the next chair. "You look pale. Did you get any sleep at all?"

Ashleigh shook her head and forked in a mouthful of food. Now that she'd tasted it, she realized she was hungry after all. "I couldn't, Mom. I was so afraid something would happen while I was asleep."

"I think you should go up and lie down for an hour."

"Oh, Mom, please, not yet. She's gotten used to me. I'm afraid she'll get scared if I'm not there, and she hasn't tried to stand by herself yet."

Ashleigh's mother reached over and laid a hand on her arm. "Okay, sweetheart."

Ashleigh's surprise at how easily her mother gave in must have shown in her face, because Mrs. Griffen went on, "I never told you about the foal I tried to save."

"No."

"I was about your age—a little younger. Seeing you yesterday made me think of it. It wasn't one of my father's Thoroughbreds—just the foal of one of the ponies on the farm. It was born premature. I wanted to spend the night out in the barn, but it was cold, and I already had the sniffles, and your grandmother wouldn't let me. The foal died during the night. It was in much worse shape than Holly's foal. It might not have made it anyway, but I couldn't help thinking that I could have saved it if I'd been there. I cried my heart out for days." Her mother looked away, deep in thought, then shook her head. "Anyway, finish your breakfast, and I'll see you out in the barn."

Ashleigh was silent.

As her mother started to rise, Rory and Caroline stumbled drowsily into the kitchen. Rory plopped down on his chair and started pouring milk into the bowl of cereal their mother had already put out. He never woke up until he ate. Caroline squinted blearily at her sister. "How's the foal?" she asked.

"All right . . . well, she's pretty much the same."

"You've got straw stuck in your hair." Caroline reached over and pulled the pieces from Ashleigh's tangled ponytail. "Did you spend the whole night in the barn?"

Ashleigh nodded and scraped the rest of the food from her plate.

"Ugh—it wouldn't be me," Caroline said. "Do you want me to bring down my tape deck so at least you can listen to some music? I've got those great new tapes."

Ashleigh smiled. She knew what a sacrifice that was for Caroline. "Thanks, Caro, but I'll be okay, and Jesse's always got a radio going during the day."

"Yeah, but all I've heard him play is classical stuff!"

Ashleigh laughed. She'd thought it was pretty strange, too, that Jesse liked classical music. He always tried to act so tough. "He told me the horses like it," Ashleigh said.

Caroline yawned and went to the cupboard for a glass. "It probably makes them sleepy, and then he has less work to do."

Ashleigh brought her plate to the sink, rinsed it, and put it in the dishwasher. She opened the refrigerator and took out a carrot and an apple for Holly. "I've got to get back," she said.

Rory had finished his cereal and was more alert. "I want to see the foal, Ashleigh."

"Not in your pajamas," Caroline told him. "The foal's not too sick for me to bring him down later, is she?" she asked Ashleigh.

"As long as he's quiet. Will you be quiet, Rory?"

"Sure." He nodded vigorously.

"She's pretty weak."

"She'll get better," Rory said with conviction.

"I hope so."

The food and the small break gave Ashleigh a second wind. When she got back to Holly's stall, her father was still kneeling beside the foal. As soon as Ashleigh opened the stall door, the foal lifted her head and made a whimpering noise.

"I think she's trying to say hello," Mr. Griffen said. Then he grew more serious. "I tried to get her up, but no dice. She still doesn't have the strength. Let's see how it goes today. But if you need any help, Ashleigh, I want you to call for one of us. You're not going to do the foal any good by getting exhausted yourself."

Ashleigh had been feeling more hopeful, but something in her father's tone made her frightened again. "I will, Dad."

The day was long and discouraging. Caroline and Rory came to look at the foal. Bill, Jesse, and April all stopped by to see how things were going, and April took Holly out for a walk around the yard. But by evening, after the other horses had been brought in, the filly still hadn't tried to stand, and Ashleigh was feeling so tired she could hardly keep her eyes open.

Her mother came by, took one look at Ashleigh's pale face, and shook her head. "You have to take a rest —no arguments. There's a cot Bill uses in the tack room. Go lie down. I'll stay with her—and I'll wake you if there's any change."

Ashleigh stumbled off. *At least I'll be close by in the barn,* she thought as she crawled onto the cot and pulled a blanket over her. She didn't wake until morning light was brightening the barn, but then she was instantly awake. She jumped off the cot and hurried to the stall.

Her father was there squatting on the straw. "I just came to relieve your mother."

Ashleigh looked anxiously at the little horse, and her father shook his head. "No change. Go up and eat. I'll stay with her till then."

Ashleigh gobbled down some cereal then hurried back so that her father could go off and do his morning chores.

When her father had gone, Ashleigh leaned over the foal and kissed the furry little head. "I know you're getting stronger. I know you could stand if you'd just believe in yourself." The foal perked up her ears and listened to Ashleigh's voice, but she didn't move.

Then Ashleigh heard a strange voice in the barn—a deep and authoritative voice. Ashleigh frowned, listening. Her father's lower tones answered. She got up and peered over the stall door, up the barn toward her parents' office. She saw her father talking to a tall man who was wearing a jacket and tie. They were standing outside Three Foot's stall, looking at the mare and her foal.

"Nice-looking colt," the tall man said. "I think we can make some plans for him."

"We've had some good foals so far, Mr. Townsend," Ashleigh's father replied. "This colt by Barbero looks good, too."

Ashleigh froze. The man her father was talking to was Clay Townsend!

"So Holly dropped a weak foal," Townsend said. "I had big hopes for that match. It's a shame. If she's that bad, we may have to put her down. Let's take a look at her."

Ashleigh spun around. They were coming toward the stall. All Ashleigh could think of was what the vet had said about Townsend being a businessman who wouldn't be willing to spend a lot of money nursing along a hopeless case.

She got down on her hands and knees and spoke in a desperate whisper. "Mr. Townsend is coming to look at you. You've got to try to stand up!"

The foal's ears perked forward, listening to the fear in Ashleigh's voice. Ashleigh reached out and rubbed her hand over the filly's neck, then backed away. "Come on, stand up. I know you can do it. See, your mother thinks so, too," she added as Holly, seeming to sense something important was happening, nickered and nudged the foal's body with her nose.

The little foal turned her head from Holly to Ashleigh. She seemed frightened. She struggled, gathering up her sticks of legs. Her body quivered with her effort. "That's it," Ashleigh urged. "Push yourself up. Try!"

But the foal couldn't make it.

Ashleigh crawled closer. "I'll help you, just a little,

but then you have to stand by yourself. Come on. Try again."

This time, as the filly tried to rise, Ashleigh slid her hands beneath the foal's belly and gave her a tiny bit of support. With a huge effort, the foal got her hind feet beneath her. Then slowly, still quivering, she straightened one foreleg, then the other, and pushed herself up. She stood, four feet planted, precariously wobbling, but on her feet. Ashleigh pulled her hands away. The foal remained standing. Ashleigh backed up to give her more room. For a moment the little filly stood perfectly still, looking around uncertainly. Then her legs gave way, and she went down in a heap.

Before Ashleigh had a chance to move or speak, the foal drew her long legs up beneath her again and with a little determined grunt, pushed up with her hind legs and straightened out her forelegs. She gave a mighty heave. She was trembling with her effort—but she was on her feet!

At that moment Mr. Townsend and Ashleigh's father stopped at the stall door. Ashleigh saw the amazed but relieved expression on her father's face.

"It looks like the filly's improving," he said to Mr. Townsend. "She's on her feet. This is my daughter Ashleigh. She's been keeping an eye on the foal."

"Hello, Mr. Townsend," Ashleigh said. Mr. Townsend nodded to her, then looked at the foal.

"Not much to her," he said.

"She's made a remarkable improvement," Mr. Griffen answered. "We really didn't hold out much hope for her, but she's obviously got heart."

"I've seen weak foals like this before," Townsend said. "They make it through, but they usually don't turn into much."

"She's got Townsend Pride's mark," Mr. Griffen said, "and Holly's certainly produced some good foals in the past."

"There is that," Mr. Townsend agreed slowly. "No other physical problems?"

"Not from what the vet can tell so far. The blood tests are fine. Her lungs are clear, heart's good. It wasn't a premature birth."

Townsend paused and frowned, watching the foal. Finally he shrugged. "Well, since she's made it this far, we might as well keep her going. With a dam and sire like hers, I'd hate to put her down, but I don't want to put a lot of time and money into saving her. You win some, you lose some. Let's have a look at the other foals."

As the men left, Ashleigh sank down on the straw. She was shaking. The foal was still standing proudly, looking at Ashleigh, perhaps expecting praise. She deserved it. She'd worked so hard to get up on her feet. If only Mr. Townsend understood how hard! He'd seemed so cold and uncaring. Was that the way he ran his farm? Her father was a businessman, too, but he'd never act like that.

Mr. Townsend's words made Ashleigh feel helpless. They reminded her that this wasn't their farm and these weren't their horses. Even her father didn't have any real control. She got up off the straw and went to the foal. The foal gently butted her head against Ashleigh's stomach, and Ashleigh ran her hand over the foal's short, tufted mane. "I think you're wonderful, girl, even if he doesn't. I'm proud of you! We'll show him. You're going to end up being the best foal he has!"

Both of Ashleigh's parents came by later that morning when Clay Townsend had left the breeding barns. "I was so glad you got her up on her feet when you did," her father said. "Try not to be too upset by what Mr. Townsend said. He's got to look at the whole picture—he can't afford to get sentimental over one foal."

"But he talked about putting her down," Ashleigh said angrily.

"Only if she didn't improve. But she is improving, isn't she?"

"You aren't the only one who's taken a special interest in this filly, either," her mother assured her. "All the hands in the barn are rooting for her."

By Sunday afternoon the little filly could wobble around on her own—just a few steps—but those steps seemed like a miracle to Ashleigh. All the healthy foals could walk a few hours after birth. Her parents, Caroline and Rory, came by to admire the filly. There were other visitors, too. During their afternoon break Bill Parks, April, Jesse, and Tom O'Brien watched as the foal demonstrated her progress by standing up and giving a shrill whinny.

"You know," Bill said, "I really didn't think I'd see this day. I didn't want to say anything at the time, Ashleigh, but I was sure she was a goner. You've worked wonders with her. Maybe we ought to call this one Ashleigh's Wonder."

April nodded in agreement.

"I'd say so, too," Tom concluded. Even Jesse gave his approval to Bill's suggestion.

Ashleigh looked at the filly. "What do you think? You *are* a wonder, aren't you?"

The foal bobbed her head so briskly that she almost tumbled over. Ashleigh had to reach out and steady her.

"That's it, then." Ashleigh laughed. "From now on, you're Wonder!" She bent down and laid her cheek against the filly's head.

6

ASHLEIGH HATED LEAVING THE FOAL THE NEXT MORNING TO GO to school. And she didn't even get a chance to talk to Linda until lunchtime, because Linda had missed the bus that morning.

The girls sat down at a table with Jennifer and Corey and another girl, Stacy, who Ashleigh didn't know very well.

"She's the most gorgeous filly—a chestnut," Ashleigh told Linda as she unwrapped her sandwich. "But she's had such a hard time." Ashleigh described everything that had happened that weekend, including Clay Townsend's inspection and what he'd said.

"But she's better now?" Linda asked worriedly.

"She's stronger and eating. My parents think she's going to be okay, except that she's going to be a lot slower than the other foals in coming along. She won't be able to go outside in the paddocks for a while. I just love her, Linda! I don't care what Mr. Townsend thinks. You'll have to come over—maybe next Saturday. Then you could spend the whole day. Wonder will have to be pretty quiet until then anyway."

"It's an awful lot of work taking care of a foal," Corey said. "Do you really want to do all that?"

Ashleigh looked at her in amazement. "Sure. Why not?"

"I'd rather wait till they're grown up, so I can ride them. That's the fun part!"

"I don't know how any of you can want to be *any*-where near horses," Stacy said with a shiver. "I've been scared to death of them since one big old monster threw me off."

"You should have gotten right back on," Jennifer told her. "Anyway, tell us about Churchill Downs, Linda."

"It was great," Linda said. "I had the most incredible time. One of our horses won his race, and one came in second, and I watched the Derby, of course. It was too bad about Townsend Victor only coming in second," she added to Ashleigh, "but it was a good race."

"I heard Bill and them talking about it," Ashleigh agreed. "But I was so busy with Wonder, I didn't get a chance to watch the race."

After lunch, Linda and Ashleigh hurried down the hall together. "I guess you'll want to go right home after school to be with Wonder," Linda said to Ashleigh. "We have a tennis match here after school to-day. I was going to ask you to come."

"It's today?" Ashleigh said. "I'd really like to see it, but I'm so worried about Wonder—"

"Don't worry. We have another at-home match next week. You can come to that."

"Okay. It's a deal."

All week Ashleigh could think only about Wonder. Each day the foal seemed to improve a little, but Ashleigh thought it might be her imagination. She had a horrible time concentrating in school and was afraid she'd flunked a math quiz on Friday. But as she got off the bus that afternoon and waved good-bye to Linda, she decided she'd worry about her math score on Monday.

She rushed to Holly and Wonder's stall as soon as she'd changed. "Happy birthday, Wonder! You're a week old today."

Hearing Ashleigh's voice, Wonder trotted across the stall and rubbed her head against Ashleigh's chest. Ashleigh bent over and gave the foal a warm hug. "I'm glad to see you, too. And guess what? Dad's decided you can go outside for the first time!"

Ashleigh's father had followed her to the stall. He leaned over the door and smiled. "By the way, Ashleigh, I picked up something for her at the store." He brought his hand from behind his back and gave

Ashleigh a tiny halter. "We didn't have one small enough in the tack room. Why don't you put it on?"

The filly perked up her ears and playfully butted Ashleigh as she carefully slipped the leather pieces over Wonder's small head and buckled the straps. "It's still a little big, but you'll grow into it. This is great, Dad!"

Mr. Griffen had collected two lead shanks. "I'll take Holly, and you take the foal," he told Ashleigh. "Wonder's not ready to go out with the other foals yet, so we'll put them in a separate paddock. She's going to be a little shy at first, and she's not used to being led, but she should follow Holly."

Ashleigh clipped the shank to Wonder's new halter. Her father did the same with Holly. The mare snorted excitedly. She knew that the lead rope meant she was going outside.

"Easy," Mr. Griffen soothed. "Just take it slow, so Wonder can keep up." He led the mare out of the stall.

Wonder whinnied frantically at seeing her mother leaving without her. "Don't worry, girl, we're going, too. Come on." Ashleigh gave a gentle tug on the lead, but Wonder didn't need any encouragement to follow her dam. She came out of the stall as fast as her spindly legs would carry her, and almost ended up in a heap on the straw.

Ashleigh tried not to laugh as she reached out and steadied the foal. Mr. Griffen kept a firm hand on

Holly. The old mare pranced and whinnied as they stepped outside. But Wonder stopped dead in her tracks, small hooves planted, and just stared. "Come on," Ashleigh coaxed. "I know it seems strange to you now, but you're going to love the paddock."

Still the filly wouldn't budge. She just gazed around with frightened eyes. Her nostrils widened as she sniffed the air, and her big ears flicked in all directions.

Ashleigh's father had continued leading Holly forward, but suddenly Holly realized her foal wasn't with her. She stopped, looked over her shoulder, and gave an encouraging call. Wonder called back. Ashleigh knew Wonder desperately wanted to go to Holly's side, but she was terrified by all the strange sights and smells. Holly called again, and Ashleigh gently urged Wonder on. The filly looked nervously around, nostrils flared, and ears and tail flicking. Finally she took several stiff-legged steps.

"Good girl," Ashleigh praised. "See, it's not so bad. Let's go catch your mom."

Thankfully the paddock was close to the barn, and Ashleigh and her father soon had Holly and Wonder inside. When they unsnapped the lead shanks and freed the horses, Holly leaned over to nuzzle Wonder, then trotted off down the paddock, shaking her head with joy at being out of the barn. Wonder tried to follow, but it was impossible for her to keep up with

71

Holly's long stride. She stumbled and fell head over heels, her legs flying in all directions.

Ashleigh started to run to her, but Mr. Griffen laid a hand on her shoulder. "Don't worry. She'll be fine. Holly just has to work off a few oats. Then she'll settle down and come back for the foal."

Wonder had already picked herself up, but as Holly cantered in wide circles, kicking up her heels, the foal stood forlorn in the middle of the paddock, looking first to Holly, then to Ashleigh, uncertain what to do. "She's scared, Dad," Ashleigh said. "I can't just leave her there."

"Wait." He pointed, and Ashleigh saw that Holly had gotten her high spirits out of her system. She trotted back to Wonder, and the two nuzzled.

"Stay and keep an eye on them for a while," Ashleigh's father said, "but I'm sure they'll be okay now."

Ashleigh had no intention of going anywhere until she was sure Wonder was all right. She climbed up on the paddock rail as Holly began grazing. Wonder, now safe by her mother's side, seemed less frightened. She looked around curiously, but she wasn't sure enough of these new surroundings to leave Holly for even a second.

From where Ashleigh sat she could see the other mares and foals in a nearby paddock. The foals raced in circles around their dams. They were healthy and full of energy. Poor Wonder looked like a lost orphan in comparison. She was so much smaller and so wobbly on her legs. But at least she was alive, Ashleigh thought—and that was more than a lot of people on the farm had expected.

The next morning Ashleigh proudly showed Linda the foal. "What do you think?" Ashleigh asked as the girls leaned their arms against the paddock rail.

"She's gorgeous!" Linda exclaimed. "Just as pretty as you said."

"Isn't she? She's still not big enough to go in with the other mares and foals yet, but it's really doing her good being outside in the fresh air."

"I wish I had a foal!" Linda sighed.

"Well, she's not really mine, even if she feels like it —it's like the horses your father trains. But I've been thinking how neat it would be if I could train her myself . . . and ride her when she's old enough. You know, like Brad Townsend does with his colt."

"So that's what you've been daydreaming about!"

Ashleigh grinned. "It's a lot more fun than thinking about dissecting a frog, or what x plus y equals."

"I thought dissecting that frog was pretty gross, too," Linda agreed.

"One of the exercise riders here is a girl," Ashleigh said. "Her name's Jilly. I've seen her ride, and she's good. April told me she wants to be a jockey. I'm going to learn to ride that well."

"You're not thinking of being a jockey?" Linda exclaimed. "You didn't tell me!"

"Well, an exercise rider for a start. I've kind of been keeping it a secret. No one would let me exercise ride yet anyway, even though I'm as tall as some of the riders. What I've been thinking is that if I can ride that well, then I'll be able to ride and train Wonder when she's old enough. Look, here they come."

Holly and Wonder had seen Ashleigh and were trotting to the fence. Wonder still had a hard time keeping up, but she was trying, and that was the important thing. The foal stuck her head through the space between the rails and nudged Ashleigh playfully.

"Hi, there." Ashleigh smiled. "Hello to you, too, Holly. Look what I've got—but you already know, don't you?" She reached in her pocket for one of the carrots that she always carried and fed it to Holly. "This is my friend Linda."

Linda rubbed a hand over Wonder's coat. "She's so friendly."

"That's probably because she's spent so much time around people since she was born. She looks more and more like her father, Townsend Pride, every day. I think she's going to have his spirit, too, even if Mr. Townsend doesn't think much of her."

"You'll fix that," Linda said.

"I'm going to try!" Ashleigh lovingly rubbed her hand over Wonder's head, then turned to Linda. "Do you want to go look at the rest of the farm now? Then we can come back and you can help me bring Holly and Wonder in before you leave."

"Sure. I'm dying to see the rest of the farm."

"Bye, guys!" Ashleigh called over her shoulder. "See you later."

Ashleigh described everything as the girls walked around the farm. She pointed out the different paddocks and barns, the training stables and rings.

"This place is so big!" Linda said when they'd reached the crest of the hill that overlooked the farm and had a bird's-eye view. "No wonder you always hear Townsend's name when it comes time for the big races. I guess he must be getting Townsend Victor ready for the Preakness in a couple of weeks."

"Yeah," Ashleigh agreed. "And the Belmont after that."

"My father's always saying how he wishes he had one of Townsend's horses to train. I don't suppose that'll ever happen, since Townsend has his own trainer."

"Mr. Maddock," Ashleigh said. "But he's away now with the horses that are racing this spring."

Ashleigh didn't need to explain much when they walked through the training area. Linda had been around a training stable all her life and knew a lot more about it than Ashleigh did, but she was impressed with the stables and track.

"My father would die for this setup," she said. "It must cost tons of money to keep up—everything's so perfect!"

"I think Mr. Townsend has a lot."

Later when the girls walked back to Holly and Wonder's paddock, they saw a tall, dark-haired boy in jeans leaning on the fence looking at the mare and foal.

"Who's that?" Linda asked curiously. "One of the grooms?"

"No," Ashleigh said. "It's Brad Townsend, the owner's son. I wonder what he's doing here."

Brad turned and saw Ashleigh and Linda.

Ashleigh felt uncomfortable, but if Brad was taking the time to look at Holly and Wonder, maybe he wasn't as obnoxious as she'd thought. "Hi," she said.

"Hi," Brad answered. "I was just cruising around, checking out all the foals. You're the one who's been taking care of this filly, aren't you? I forgot your name."

"Ashleigh Griffen. This is my friend Linda March. Linda, Brad Townsend. Wonder's really coming along, isn't she?" Ashleigh looked fondly at Wonder, who was trotting along beside Holly toward the paddock gate.

Brad shrugged. "I suppose, but I doubt she'll ever make it to the track."

"What do you mean?" Ashleigh asked.

"She's a runt."

Ashleigh bristled. "She'll catch up."

Brad lazily brushed his fingers through his hair. "I wouldn't count on it. My father doesn't think much of her. From what he says, she'll be one of the horses he sends to auction."

Ashleigh felt the color draining from her face. "No!"

"Wanna bet?"

"I wouldn't waste my money!"

Brad turned and pointed to the paddock where the other mares and foals were grazing. "There's the foal to keep an eye on—Three Foot's. You can already see he's got good conformation. My father's told me I can train him. He'll be a winner."

"And Wonder will, too!"

"Come on." Brad smirked. "Be serious. It's your time if you want to waste it, but I can tell you haven't been around a training farm for long. That filly is definitely not a winner. See ya." He turned and sauntered off.

Ashleigh swung around to Linda. "He can't mean it," she said angrily. "He's just trying to show off—pretend he knows so much about racing. Mr. Townsend won't sell Wonder!" But Ashleigh felt a sick feeling of dread.

Linda stared after Brad and shook her blond curls vigorously. "Don't pay any attention to him. He's being a jerk."

Ashleigh wasn't reassured. Could Brad be right? Maybe his father *had* already decided that Wonder should go. From what Ashleigh had seen of Mr. Townsend, she could believe it was possible. "If they sell Wonder, I'll just die, Linda!"

"How could they decide so soon?" Linda asked. "She's only a week old! I think he was just trying to be a big shot."

But Ashleigh couldn't get Brad's words out of her mind, and that night she had a hard time sleeping. Caroline finally called over to her, "Stop tossing and turning. You're making the bed squeak and keeping me awake!"

"Sorry," Ashleigh whispered.

For the rest of the week it did nothing but rain, and that didn't improve Ashleigh's mood. It was too wet to leave the horses out, especially the foals, but they all needed exercise. All the hands in the foaling barn wrapped themselves in slickers and the mares and foals in light blankets and took turns walking the horses. They walked the hardier horses outside on the drive. But Ashleigh didn't want to take that risk with Wonder. She didn't want the foal getting wet and chilled, and her father and Bill Parks agreed. Instead she walked Holly and Wonder up and down the long barn aisle, but even the air in the barn felt damp.

Finally the rain ended. The sun and a fresh breeze dried the soggy paddocks. Holly and Wonder seemed just fine when Ashleigh put them out in their paddock in the morning. They both frisked across the grass, glad to be out of the barn.

That day Ashleigh stayed after school to watch Linda's tennis match. When she got home, she noticed that Wonder seemed listless. She stayed by Holly's side, hanging her head. Ashleigh climbed over the fence and walked over. Wonder looked at Ashleigh with her usual affection and trust, but something wasn't right.

Ashleigh hugged her. "What's wrong?"

The filly gave a little grunt and coughed.

Then Ashleigh noticed that Wonder felt hot—too hot—and her nose was running. Horses didn't get human colds, but they had their own coldlike viruses. Wonder was showing all the symptoms.

Ashleigh ran to the paddock gate, collected Holly's and Wonder's leads, and led them both to the barn. "Dad!" she cried. "Come quick! I think Wonder's sick!"

Her father stuck his head out of his office at the end of the barn. "What's wrong?"

"Her nose is running, she's hot, and she's coughing."

He hurried down the barn aisle. Ashleigh already had the mare and foal in the stall. Her father knelt beside Wonder. He shook his head. "Keep her warm. Get a blanket over her. I'll call the vet."

Ashleigh remembered Dr. James's warning about Wonder being susceptible to disease. She ran to the tack room and found a clean blanket. Back in the stall, she wrapped it around Wonder. The foal had dropped down onto the bedding and curled up. Holly was nudging her, sensing something was wrong. In a moment Ashleigh's father returned. "We're lucky. Dr. James is over in the training barn. He'll be right here. She was fine this morning, wasn't she?" her father asked.

"Yes. She was trotting around."

"You caught it early then." He rubbed his hand over Ashleigh's hair. "We'll see what we can do."

"Dr. James said because she was so small and weak . . ." Ashleigh couldn't finish.

"You just keep holding her and talking to her. She knows and trusts you and that's the best medicine she could have right now." But her father looked concerned, and Ashleigh knew he was thinking of the virus that had swept through Edgardale.

A few minutes later Dr. James appeared. He went right to the foal and lifted the blanket. Ashleigh scooted out of his way, clenching her cold hands together. The vet's examination seemed to take forever.

"Influenza," he finally said. He looked up at Holly. "How's the mare?"

"She seems fine."

"As you know, it's highly contagious, but the filly's

bound to be more susceptible than the mare. Better quarantine them both and keep an eye on the other horses. We don't want it spreading through the barn. I'm going to give her a shot to control the fever and any muscle stiffness. Keep her warm and dry and make sure she nurses. If we've caught it in time, there may not be any complications."

"Do you think she'll be all right?" Ashleigh said, her voice trembling.

"I'd say maybe she has a chance."

After Dr. James left, Mr. Griffen readied the stall at the far end of the barn that was separated from the other stalls by a wall and a passageway. It was only used for contagious animals. When it was ready, Ashleigh brought Holly and Wonder over. Wonder didn't want to get up off the bedding and had to be coaxed to walk the distance.

"I'll get April or Jesse to clean and disinfect the old stall," Mr. Griffen said. "We can't have this spreading. It's a good thing Holly and Wonder were in a separate paddock. I'll have them bring Holly's feed, too. You stay here and keep the foal warm. Get her up to nurse if you can. Otherwise we'll have to force-feed her."

Ashleigh cuddled Wonder close, and for the long hours that followed she stayed by the foal's side. After all her work, she wondered if she was going to lose the foal. She managed to get Wonder up to eat once, but the filly had no appetite and soon collapsed back on the bedding. Wonder had grown several inches taller in the past two weeks, but she still seemed like a fragile bundle when Ashleigh lay down beside her to keep her warm. Her back was less than two feet long, and Ashleigh could easily encircle Wonder's rib cage with her arm.

Ashleigh couldn't see the rest of the barn from the isolation stall, but from time to time she heard worried voices, then the commotion of the other mares and foals being brought in. Jesse came by with Holly's feed and water. He looked at Wonder and shook his head.

Ashleigh's parents were worried about another virus epidemic and spent the evening in the barn, checking horses and disinfecting. They were so busy, they hardly seemed to notice Ashleigh.

Her mother finally stopped by and looked over the stall door. She had wrapped her blond hair in a red bandanna, but loose ends were slipping out around her face, and she looked tired.

"You're all right?" she asked Ashleigh. "We want to watch the other foals. Two of them have a slight fever. Run up to the house and get something to eat when you can."

"I will, Mom," Ashleigh said. She knew what her parents were going through. She'd already seen it once before at Edgardale, and if two of the other foals were running fevers, it wasn't good.

April came by and relieved her for a while. "How are the other horses?" Ashleigh asked.

April shook her head. "Your mom and dad are with them. I'm not sure. We've been moving horses all night, trying to isolate the sick foals." She hesitated. "Is this the kind of thing you had happen before?"

Ashleigh cringed, then nodded. "Yes. But it's not really that bad yet."

April groaned, but shooed Ashleigh off.

The hours after she'd eaten passed even more slowly for Ashleigh. For a while Wonder seemed to grow worse instead of better. Ashleigh could hear voices from the rest of the barn, but she didn't know what was happening. That frightened her more. Was the virus spreading? Were other horses getting sick? Was it going to be Edgardale all over again?

Finally, late in the evening, Ashleigh's parents and Bill Parks came by to check the foal. Ashleigh had gotten Wonder to nurse briefly once more, but after that the foal refused. They all conferred and decided to wait awhile before taking further steps with Wonder. They had enough on their minds trying to keep the virus from spreading.

Ashleigh gently stroked Wonder's coat, speaking soothingly to her. Once or twice the foal grunted in discomfort and tried to lift her head. "I'm here, Wonder. So's your mom. We'll make you better."

From time to time Holly nickered and nuzzled her

foal. She trusted Ashleigh and seemed to know that Ashleigh was doing her best for Wonder. Eventually Holly lowered herself down on the bedding of the big stall and settled for the night. She lay with her head close to her foal and Ashleigh, keeping a gentle eye on them both. Somehow she knew to keep her legs out of reach.

"We'll be all right . . . we'll *all* be all right," Ashleigh whispered. She laid one hand on Wonder's warm body and the other on Holly's neck, and leaned back against the side of the stall. Her eyes felt so heavy, but she couldn't sleep . . . not tonight . . . she couldn't . . .

7

ASHLEIGH WOKE SUDDENLY, SENSING SOMETHING WAS WRONG. She jerked up and looked around. This wasn't her bedroom. But it wasn't the stall either! There was a dim light, and she smelled hay and horses and leather. She was on the cot in the tack room. But how had she gotten here? She threw off the blanket that was covering her and jumped from the cot.

She quickly staggered out into the main aisle of the barn, then around toward the isolation stall. Except for the gentle snort of a sleeping horse, everything was perfectly still. The ceiling light was shining outside the isolation stall. Her stomach balled in a knot of dread as she looked over the stall door. There was Holly asleep, and Wonder curled on the bedding—thank heavens! But someone was crouched next to Wonder. Ashleigh couldn't believe her eyes. It was Charlie Burke!

Ashleigh stared at the old man. "What are you doing here?"

"Came by and saw you sound asleep," he said gruffly. "I thought maybe you all needed a hand. Your parents were with some of the other horses. The filly's okay, if you're wondering."

"Did you put me on the cot?"

"Seemed the least I could do . . . spell you awhile. And old Holly here knows me. Ought to. I trained her when she was a two-year-old. She's a fine old mare. We have an attachment, you could say, and I've taken an interest in this foal of hers. I've been keeping an eye on you, too. Admire your spunk."

Ashleigh was astounded. Her mouth had fallen open, and she quickly snapped it shut.

Charlie Burke didn't give her time to comment. "The foal's had a rough time of it, but I think we can save her."

"You do?"

"With the two of us keeping an eye on her, I don't see why not. I just don't want it getting around the stables that I'm spending too much time with the filly —getting soft."

"Why would anyone think that?" Ashleigh asked.

Charlie frowned. "Just don't you say anything."

"I won't," Ashleigh promised.

"Let's get to work," the old trainer said in a businesslike tone. "I don't think we can get her to nurse on her own, but I think we can get some milk down her. Here, you hold her for a bit. I want to mix up a little something."

Ashleigh went into the stall. She could hardly believe that Charlie was helping her, but she did what he said. Wonder was awake, yet she lay perfectly still, too sick to lift her head. Ashleigh fought back a feeling of panic. "Poor baby," she said. "We're going to make you better." She gently placed her hand on Wonder's neck.

Charlie returned a few minutes later carrying a small plastic bucket and a feeding bottle. "I mixed up some milk substitute," he explained. "I'll show you what to do." He squatted down by Wonder's head and dipped his fingers in the bucket. Then he carefully opened Wonder's mouth and rubbed his fingers inside. The foal weakly licked up the milk. Charlie quickly inserted the nipple of the bottle, but Wonder spat it out. Charlie sighed. "Looks like we'll have to do it the hard way for now." He dipped his fingers in the milk again and rubbed them in Wonder's mouth. Then he told Ashleigh to try.

She did, and gradually over the next hour they got Wonder to swallow half of the milk in the bucket. "That'll do her for now," Charlie said. "If she won't drink from the bottle tomorrow, we might have to use a stomach tube. Better let her rest. You keep holding her while I clean up this stall a little and get some feed and water for Holly." The old man set to work cleaning out dirty bedding. Holly was up on her feet now. After checking her foal, she stood to one side of the stall out of Charlie's way.

"Thanks for helping me, Mr. Burke," Ashleigh said. "I couldn't have done all this myself."

"None of this Mr. Burke stuff. Charlie's just fine. And it's no trouble. They don't seem to have much other use for me around here anymore."

"But you've trained dozens of horses," Ashleigh protested.

"More like hundreds. But Maddock, he's got his own ideas. Doesn't want any advice from the old man. Thinks I'm too old to know what I'm doing anymore. I've been put out to pasture."

"That isn't fair. I think you know what you're doing."

For the first time the old man gave a hint of a smile. "That so?"

"Right after we first moved here, I was watching the training one morning, and I heard you saying something about the way Brad Townsend was treating his colt."

"I remember. Rough-handling him—trying to show the colt who's master by muscling him around. That's Maddock's style—not mine. Always say you get more with sugar than vinegar."

"Mr. Maddock is mean to the horses?"

"Naw. No decent trainer'd ever abuse an animal. Still, some think a horse learns faster from punishment than reward. You remember that girl Jilly, who rode that same day? She had some trouble with her mount, too. It's just high spirits. Those young horses like playing around when they first get out in the morning. But you noticed she never laid a whip on him. She understood what the horse was feeling. She talked him down—used her voice and a gentler hand."

"I want to be an exercise rider someday," Ashleigh couldn't resist saying.

Charlie scowled and lifted another pitchfork of bedding. "Do you now?" he finally muttered. "Times are changing. I've got nothing against women in the business, but it's a dangerous sport for a woman."

Ashleigh wasn't going to let him get away with that excuse. "It's just as dangerous for men!"

"Hmph!" Charlie grunted.

Ashleigh noticed that light was beginning to filter through the high stable windows. Charlie had finished seeing to Holly, and he leaned against the stall door. "Think you can manage on your own for a while?" he asked.

Ashleigh nodded.

"I'll have a word with your father, tell him what I've done with the substitute feeding, but don't say anything to the other hands. I'll be back later today."

He patted Wonder and Holly, then slipped out of the stall.

"Thanks, Charlie," Ashleigh called softly after him, but he was already gone. For a moment Ashleigh wondered if she'd been dreaming, but there was the bucket and bottle they'd used to feed Wonder. And amazingly the foal did seem a little better. She seemed more comfortable and not nearly so hot.

Soon Ashleigh heard noises from the rest of the barn, signaling the start of another day. Horses whinnied and stomped, waiting for their morning meal. Jesse had put his classical music on the radio. Her parents came to the stall.

They both looked concerned. "We just talked to Charlie Burke," her father said. "He told us he'd given you a hand. That was good of him, and he did the right thing."

"He was a big help, Dad."

"I'm sure he was. He's had a lot of experience and knows his stuff. We seem to have gotten through the night okay. The foals that were showing symptoms seem better. We can't be sure yet, but none of the mares seem infected."

"I think it's time you took a break," her mother added. "I'll keep an eye on Wonder. You go up to the house, have breakfast, and get cleaned up."

Ashleigh rose stiffly and brushed off her clothes, careful not to disturb Wonder too much. "It's going to be all right? It's not going to be like before?" she asked.

"We think it's going to be all right," her father said. "Go ahead and have some breakfast."

"I'll be right back," Ashleigh told the foal. Wonder lifted her head and gave a tiny squeal. Ashleigh felt so tired, she couldn't think straight. "I don't have to go to school today—do I?" she asked her parents.

"After what we all went through last night, no," her mother said exhaustedly. "But you can't miss too much school—tomorrow, you'll have to go."

The few hours of sleep she'd gotten were enough to keep Ashleigh going. Bill, April, and Jesse pitched in to do what they could for Holly, although they had to be careful not to spread the influenza to any of the other horses. Any buckets used for the mare and foal and any other questionable foals had to be sterilized, and anyone who touched them had to wash carefully.

Although she was too sick to stand, Wonder had finally started taking milk from the bottle, and by the time Charlie came to relieve Ashleigh in the early evening, Wonder was definitely improving.

"She's got more energy, Charlie," Ashleigh told the trainer, "and she doesn't seem as hot. I think we could get her to nurse if we held her."

"Why don't you let me take care of that? You need a

good night's sleep. Go on home, and I'll see you in the morning."

This time Ashleigh went without an argument. The thought of her warm, soft bed seemed awfully nice. And she'd have to go to school in the morning. Her mother would never let her miss another day. She was asleep as soon as her head touched the pillow.

For the next two days she and Charlie took their turns with Wonder. Ashleigh hated leaving the foal to go to school, but at least she had Linda to talk to. Fortunately the flu virus didn't spread. The foals her parents had worried about recovered. The other mares and foals remained healthy and strong. Ashleigh could see the relief on her parents' faces.

When Ashleigh returned from school in midweek, Wonder was standing in her stall. Charlie was there with her.

"Not bad, eh?" He smiled. "Did it all by herself, too. I just came by to check her out, and there she was. We've got the flu beat."

Ashleigh felt tears come to her eyes as she hugged the foal.

"I thought you'd be happy," Charlie said.

Mr. Griffen looked in over the stall door after Charlie had gone. "Well, looks like she'll make it—thanks to you and Charlie. We've been really lucky this time. The other foals are fine, and none of the mares picked it up. Wonder was the worst. That old guy thinks a lot of your courage. Of course, he'd never tell you that to your face."

Ashleigh smiled. She knew Charlie wasn't the type to give a lot of compliments.

"This has been a real setback for Wonder," her father added. "You're going to have to take it slow with her."

"That's what Charlie said. He told me we'd have to keep her quiet for a while, then just exercise her a little at a time. She won't be able to go in with the other mares and foals."

"It's a shame. She was coming along so well before she got sick. I was thinking of moving her and Holly into the other paddock, but now we'll have to wait." Her father paused. "I hope this isn't getting to be too much for you, Ashleigh. You're spreading yourself pretty thin."

"No, Dad! I can do it. I want to! I don't feel tired at all."

"I hope you're right."

For the first time since Wonder had gotten sick, Ashleigh could leave her and Holly without worry when she went in for the night. Unfortunately, she had time to think of other things, too—like homework. She'd let it go because Wonder seemed so much more important. Now Ashleigh had a book report due the next day and two tests to study for. School would be out for summer vacation soon. If she came home with a bad report card, her parents would say she was spending too much time with the horses. She couldn't let that happen. That night she spread her books out on her bed and frantically went to work.

8

"WHEW!" ASHLEIGH SAID WITH RELIEF. "MY REPORT CARD'S not as bad as I thought—only two *C*'s. How'd you do?" she asked Linda.

"I got an *A* in gym!" Linda exclaimed.

"You should. You're so good in tennis." Ashleigh stood up from her desk and slid her report card into her notebook. She couldn't believe it was the last day of school—finally! The only bad part of it was that Linda was going off with her father to the New York races for the first half of the summer. "I'm going to miss you," Ashleigh said. "I almost wish you weren't going. No, I shouldn't say that—you'll have a great time."

"Yeah, and you'll have Wonder to keep you busy."

Ashleigh smiled at the thought. The filly was healthy again, and all the staff in the breeding barns had shown up the day before to watch Wonder take her first walk outside since coming down with the flu.

"I'll be back before the end of summer anyway," Linda added.

"Write and tell me all about it. I don't want to have to wait till you get back. Promise?"

"Promise." Linda grinned.

The dismissal bell rang. Ashleigh, Linda, and the other twenty kids in their homeroom jumped out of their chairs with shouts of joy. "Have a good summer, everyone!" the homeroom teacher, Mrs. Katz, called over the bedlam. Ashleigh and Linda grabbed their backpacks and ran for the door.

"No, Rory, that's not the way to groom her." Ashleigh laughed. "And Wonder, stop trying to eat the brush!"

Ashleigh was taking her turn watching Rory. Caroline hadn't wanted to spend her whole summer babysitting, and Ashleigh didn't blame her, but Rory could be a handful. She'd only kept him in the stall with her that early July morning by giving him the special privilege of grooming Wonder.

Unfortunately, Rory's grooming methods were pretty casual. He totally ignored Wonder's head and legs, and Wonder didn't help. She thought it was a game and kept twisting her head around to nibble at the soft brush he held, and to butt his arm with her

96

nose. Bits of bedding still clung to Wonder's legs and belly when Rory was finished, but Wonder affectionately nuzzled his ear with her soft lips.

Rory went off into a fit of giggles. "That tickles, Wonder. You're silly." He pushed Wonder's head away. "She likes me a lot, Ashleigh, doesn't she?"

"Uh-huh. You know, Wonder's got a big day ahead of her. Dad's decided it's time she and Holly went into the paddock with the other mares and foals."

"Can I lead her?" he asked excitedly.

"I'll let you help hold the shank if you promise not to jump around too much. Here comes Dad now."

Ashleigh was worried about the move. Wonder had grown since recovering from the flu. Her head was as high as Ashleigh's shoulder, but she still looked frail. "Are you sure she'll be all right?" she asked her father as they led the horses toward the paddock. "She's so small compared to the other foals. Won't they push her around?"

"You're beginning to sound like an overprotective mother," her father teased. "It'll be an adjustment for her, but she'll be just fine. She needs to be out with the other horses and learn to fend for herself."

After they'd freed Holly and Wonder, Mr. Griffen went back to the barn, but Ashleigh and Rory stood anxiously at the paddock fence. Charlie joined them.

Ashleigh could see that Wonder was terrified. She clung to Holly's side for protection as the other foals curiously approached to investigate the new arrival. All of them were several inches taller than Wonder at the shoulders, and their backs had begun to lengthen. Wonder still had the awkward, long-legged gangliness of a young foal.

They nudged Wonder playfully at first, but she didn't know what to make of them. Wonder had only been around humans and Holly, and she wasn't big enough or strong enough to keep up with the other foals' roughhousing. She cowered closer to Holly. Holly did what she could to protect her foal. She chased away the bullies with nips and kicks, but she could only do so much.

"They're going to hurt Wonder!" Rory cried.

Ashleigh turned quickly to Charlie for his opinion.

"No, they won't. She's feeling strange, but she'll catch on. Just give 'em a few minutes."

"But the others are so much bigger," Ashleigh said. "Do you think Wonder will ever catch up?"

"In time, and Holly'll take care of her. Look."

Holly had decided it was time for a drink at the water trough. Half a dozen mares were already at the trough. Holly pushed right through, laying back her ears in warning to those who didn't move. Wonder followed along close to her mother's side, and soon the mare and foal had the trough to themselves.

"These horses have their own pecking order," Charlie explained with a grin. "Holly's what you'd call one of the boss mares. She's not going to let any of the others get in her way, and the others know better than to mess with her. It's a good lesson for Wonder. Holly's a tough old lady." Charlie chuckled. "But you want to see that in a racehorse. It's a sign that they won't let another horse get the better of them on the track. I think little Wonder may have inherited some of that fight from her mother."

"Really?" Ashleigh asked. It was hard to believe, looking at Wonder now. While Wonder had been recovering from the flu, she'd lost a lot of ground. If anything, Wonder looked more like a runt than ever.

Yet a few days later, when Ashleigh went to the paddock fence to watch, she could see that Wonder was learning how to stand up for herself. She wasn't big enough to push the other foals around, but she didn't let them push her around, either. She stood her ground, and when the other foals got too rough, Wonder sent a well-aimed kick in their direction.

"Good for you!" Ashleigh called proudly over the fence. At the sound of Ashleigh's voice, Wonder came trotting over with a whinny of greeting and pushed her head through the top two rails of the fence. Ashleigh rubbed the filly's ears. "You're still my girl, aren't you?"

Ashleigh's father walked up beside her. "She's doing okay, isn't she?" Then he added cheerfully, "Come with me for a minute. I've got something to show you."

Ashleigh was mystified, but her father wouldn't give her any hints as he led her around the barn toward the training area. He stopped at one of the paddocks. There were two horses inside, an Appaloosa mare, who had that breed's distinctive liver-and-white spotting, and a big, elegantly built bay horse.

"I finally found some riding horses for us. There you go." He smiled and pointed to the bay.

Ashleigh stared at the horse, then her father. "For me? To ride?"

"He sure is. His name's Dominator."

"But he looks like a Thoroughbred!"

"He is." Her father laughed. "An old gelding. He's been retired from racing for years. Bill thought he'd make a good mount for you. He's even-tempered and isn't going to pull any crazy stuff. Townsend's daughter used to trailride him before she got married. The mare's ours to ride, too. Her name's Belle, but I thought you'd like to try a Thoroughbred for a change."

"Oh, wow! I sure would!" Ashleigh gasped. She'd known her father would find them some riding horses, but she'd never expected hers to be a Thoroughbred! She was so thrilled, she didn't know what to say.

April came toward the paddock grinning and carrying a saddle. "Not bad," she called as she went into the paddock and started tacking up Dominator.

"Why don't you try him out in the paddock first," Mr. Griffen said. "Then you can take him out around the farm. But keep in sight of the barns and the training area until you get used to him."

"I promise!" Ashleigh was already hurrying over to April and Dominator. She held out her hand to the horse and let him sniff it. Then she rubbed her hand over his neck and spoke quietly to him, letting him know she was a friend. She went to his side, slid her foot into the stirrup, and mounted.

Ashleigh could hardly believe she was sitting in the saddle on a Thoroughbred. Now she could really practice her riding, so that when Wonder was old enough Ashleigh *would* be ready to ride her!

April stepped away, and Ashleigh urged the horse into a walk around the paddock. Dominator might have been old, but he still moved with smooth grace. And he'd been well trained. He was responsive to the slightest touch on the reins or pressure of Ashleigh's legs. Ashleigh loosened the reins and squeezed lightly with her legs, and Dominator broke into a trot. She took him several times around the paddock, then stopped him by the fence where her father and April were standing.

She was so excited, she felt butterflies in her stomach. "He's great, Dad!"

"Ready to head out?" her father asked. Ashleigh nodded, and her father swung open the paddock gate.

"I'll be careful."

"I know you will. Have fun."

Her father didn't have to worry about that! As they trotted along between the white fences, horses in the paddocks lifted their heads and whinnied. A younger horse might have been distracted by the cries, but Dominator remained calm. At the crest of the hill, Ashleigh turned the horse to the right and urged him into a canter over the thick grass. Dominator's long legs seemed to eat up the ground.

What a difference it made, riding a Thoroughbred! Stardust had always put her heart into their rides, but her gaits had never been so smooth, her strides so powerful and effortless. The breeze lifted Ashleigh's hair as she and Dominator whipped by the white fenceposts. She felt tempted to urge Dominator into a gallop, but she didn't dare push him to that speed until she was sure of the trail ahead. Even at a canter, she felt like she was flying as they swung around a bend in the path.

As they raced along, she couldn't help dreaming of the day when Wonder was fully grown. She imagined herself in the saddle, crouched low over the filly's neck, racing along at a full gallop!

They were still high on the crest of the hill, and below Ashleigh could see the training stables, the oval of the ring, and the green paddocks spread out around them. She felt like she was on top of the world.

When the trail began to dip back down toward the barns, Ashleigh slowed Dominator and trotted him along under a canopy of trees. She no longer had a sweeping view of the farm and wasn't sure exactly where they were, but the path they were on was well used and marked by hoof prints. She urged Dominator back into a canter, and the horse eagerly picked up his pace.

As they rounded a tree-lined bend, she saw another rider cantering toward them. The horse looked a lot like the colt Brad Townsend had been riding, and as they drew closer, she recognized Brad in the saddle.

Ashleigh felt so happy and excited that she lifted her hand in a friendly wave and even smiled at Brad as the two horses swept past each other. She couldn't help feeling a nudge of satisfaction, too, to have Brad see her on the back of a Thoroughbred.

She giggled when she saw his expression. He stared at her wide-eyed. He sure hadn't expected to see *her* cantering along on Dominator. But the horses were moving too quickly for him to do more than gape at her for an instant. *That'll show you, snob!* she thought as she cantered away. *I can ride, too!*

The space between the fences was wider here, and the ground was level. Again, Ashleigh was tempted to put Dominator into a gallop, but through a break in the trees she saw stable buildings ahead and knew they were approaching the training area. As they drew closer, she slowed Dominator to a trot, then a walk.

Stable hands looked up curiously as they passed by the front of the training stable yard. Dominator perked up his ears and pranced a few steps in excitement. "You remember this from when you used to race, don't you?" Ashleigh asked. "I'll bet you missed having someone take you riding. Hanging around in a paddock all the time must get pretty boring."

One of the grooms called out to her, "That's old Dominator, isn't it?"

Ashleigh nodded and smiled.

"Nice to see someone riding him again, but that's a lot of horse for you."

"Oh, no! He's got beautiful manners. He's a great old horse."

Ashleigh waved to the groom and headed Dominator away from the stable. "See you later."

Her father saw her returning and came over as she dismounted near the paddock and started to untack the horse.

"I can tell by your face that you've had a good ride."

"Incredible!" Ashleigh beamed. "This was absolutely the best surprise, Dad! I'm so happy!"

Ashleigh was sore that night after not having ridden for so long. She soaked away her aches in a hot tub, but the ride had been worth it. All she wanted to do was practice and practice on Dominator, until she was as good as the other exercise riders on the farm—good enough to have a chance of riding Wonder.

And during the next few days, Ashleigh *did* practice —until her muscles started getting in condition again, and she and Dominator were working like a pair. By the end of the week she'd galloped him down the lane for the first time. As she rode back from the ride, her face was glowing from her achievement. Dominator was excited, too, prancing and tossing his head. But as they reached the breeding area, Ashleigh looked over to the mares' and foals' paddock, and suddenly pulled Dominator up.

Mr. Townsend, Mr. Maddock, and her father were standing by the paddock fence, looking at the foals.

She nervously watched as the men walked slowly along the fence. They paused from time to time, pointing to one foal or another and talking among themselves. She couldn't hear what the men were saying, but she could see their faces. She saw Townsend and Maddock nodding and sometimes smiling.

But when her father pointed out Wonder, they both frowned and shook their heads. Her father kept talking. Mr. Townsend shrugged, obviously unimpressed, then they all moved farther down along the fence.

Ashleigh hated to ask her father what they'd said, but that night at dinner she decided she had to know.

"I saw Mr. Townsend and Mr. Maddock looking at the foals, Dad. They didn't like Wonder, did they?"

Her father looked over, then shook his head. "I have to be honest. No, they weren't impressed. They're looking for the foals with the most potential. In this business you can't afford to take risks. Wonder doesn't look like a good risk right now. That may change . . ."

"It will!"

"I think you've done an outstanding job nursing the filly, but you have to be prepared for the worst, too. Townsend may eventually decide to sell Wonder off."

"No! That's what Brad told me, but I thought he was just trying to show off. I didn't believe him."

"Brad told you that?" Caroline said in surprise.

"They can't sell Wonder!" Rory cried. "She's too special."

"When do they sell the horses?" Ashleigh asked in a shaky voice.

"There are weanling auctions in the fall, then after the first of the year the yearling auctions start. But let's not get upset yet," Mr. Griffen said quickly. "The filly may very well stay on the farm. I just want you to understand the realities, Ashleigh. I don't want you to get your hopes up so high that you'll be hurt later."

"But Wonder really hasn't had a chance yet!"

"I know. But there's time. You have the rest of the summer."

Ashleigh saw Caroline glance at her. She knew what Caroline was thinking—that Mr. Townsend wouldn't keep Wonder. But after nursing and caring for the filly, Ashleigh felt like Wonder belonged to her, not to Mr. Townsend!

Ashleigh rushed through clearing the table and stacking the dishes in the dishwasher, then hurried outside. She wanted to talk to Charlie and see what he thought. He'd probably be in the training stables, talking to the grooms. Ashleigh checked out one of the stable blocks and didn't see him, but in the second she found him standing outside talking to one of the hands.

It was still a big secret in the training area that Charlie had helped her with Wonder, so Ashleigh waited a few yards away. The groom had his back toward her and didn't know she was there. When Charlie lifted his head and rearranged his floppy hat, Ashleigh waved to him and motioned for him to meet her around the side of the barn.

Charlie nodded lazily and kept talking to the groom.

Ashleigh ran around the side of the stable and waited. A few minutes later Charlie appeared.

Ashleigh began speaking in a frantic jumble of words. "Mr. Townsend came around the paddocks this morning and looked at the foals. He and Mr. Maddock didn't like Wonder, Charlie. They may sell her."

"Hold on," Charlie said calmly. "Nobody's selling anything today."

She told Charlie about the men's reaction to Wonder and what her parents had said.

"Like your parents told you, there's time. Won't be any decisions made for a while yet. Townsend never sends anything to the fall auctions unless it's a mare and foal pair, and Holly's too old to sell. You won't have anything to worry about until winter, when the yearling auctions start." He shifted his hat back on his head and thought for a moment. "There's a few things you could do to help Wonder along. She's two months now, isn't she? Old enough to start creep feeding."

"What's that?"

"We'll start giving her a little grain mix—not too much. Your father's got some in the feed room. It's a concentrate that's got extra protein and minerals—it'll help supplement the mare's milk. They usually don't start foals on it until they're three months old, but the filly's getting close to that and could use the extra boost. Just a little, though, to get her started. And we'd better tell your father what we're up to. Come on. I'll walk over there with you now."

They found Ashleigh's father in his office. Charlie explained what he had in mind, and Mr. Griffen nodded. "I should have thought of it myself. Go ahead, Charlie. You know where everything is, and you can show Ashleigh the right mix and quantity."

Ashleigh and Charlie headed off to the feed room. The old man showed Ashleigh the mix and the amounts she should measure out. When Ashleigh and Charlie entered the stall, Wonder came over and nudged Ashleigh with affectionate playfulness. Charlie took hold of Holly's lead so she wouldn't go after Wonder's food herself.

"Look what we've got for you." Ashleigh grinned as she set the bucket of feed down on the floor near Wonder.

Wonder looked curiously at the bucket, then dropped her elegant little head and tentatively sniffed the contents. She gazed at Ashleigh uncertainly.

"Go ahead." Ashleigh laughed. "It's food. You'll love it."

Still Wonder hesitated.

"Maybe I should give you a taste," Ashleigh said. She reached in the bucket and dipped her fingers in the soupy mix. Then she held her fingers to Wonder's mouth and waited until the filly delicately tasted the new food.

Wonder immediately squealed with delight and gently nibbled Ashleigh's hand, looking for more.

"Good, isn't it?" Ashleigh encouraged. "But you'll have to eat from the bucket to get the rest." She lifted the bucket and held it under Wonder's nose. Wonder quickly understood, and in a second dipped her head into the bucket and dug in.

"Good girl!" Ashleigh said, giving Wonder a hug. "She likes it, Charlie!"

"Yup." Charlie nodded, watching Wonder eat. "Now we'll just have to wait and see if it adds any meat to her bones."

9

DURING THE HOT, LAZY DAYS OF AUGUST, ASHLEIGH STARTED taking Wonder and Holly for long walks around the farm. Rory usually tagged along, riding bareback on his new pony. Their parents had found the pony at a neighboring farm. Rory had named him Moe II. He was fat and furry and wouldn't go faster than a trot, but Rory loved him.

One afternoon Caroline came along with them. She led Holly while Ashleigh took Wonder's shank. They both kept an eye on Rory as he trotted ahead.

"Why didn't you ride Belle?" Ashleigh asked her sister.

"You know I don't like riding anymore—ever since that horse at Edgardale spooked on me."

"He only bolted because that car backfired. You're a good rider."

111

Caroline shook her head. "I get too nervous—I'm scared it could happen again."

"Look at me—no hands!" Rory called from in front of them.

"Don't do that!" Caroline called back with a touch of panic. "The pony might run away."

"Naw." Rory laughed. "He's too lazy."

"Just the same," Ashleigh told him, "wait till you're in a paddock before you practice balancing."

Rory made a face and picked up the reins.

"You're going to love this place I found for swimming," Ashleigh told Caroline. "It's great."

"I could sure use a swim," Caroline answered, wiping droplets of sweat from her forehead. "It's getting hot."

"There it is," Ashleigh said as they came over a low hill. The rippling water of the stream sparkled in the sunlight and widened into a pool under some weeping willows. Rory kicked Moe into a jouncy trot. The pony splashed right into the stream, and Rory let out a peal of laughter.

"Wow, that looks good!" Caroline said. "Okay, Holly, let's go wading." Caroline led the old mare forward, and the two of them splashed in behind Rory.

Ashleigh pulled Wonder ahead, too. "Come on, girl, you'll love it!" The filly readily followed Ashleigh, but at the water's edge she planted her feet firmly and skidded to a sudden stop. Ashleigh felt the jerk on the lead shank but couldn't stop herself in time—she tripped and landed flat on her face! She flailed around, then came up spitting out a mouthful of water. Caroline and Rory were laughing their heads off.

Ashleigh pushed her wet hair out of her eyes. She couldn't help laughing, too. "That's one way to get wet!" She turned to Wonder, who was still standing stiff-legged on the bank, looking baffled, but curious. Ashleigh gave a tug on the shank. "You're not going to stay dry after you got *me* soaking wet." When the filly wouldn't budge, Ashleigh stepped back up on the bank, got behind Wonder, and pushed. Startled, the filly leaped forward and landed knee deep in the stream. She let out a shrill whinny, but Ashleigh was right by her side, reassuring her. "See, it's not so bad."

"Come on, Wonder!" Rory called from the back of his pony.

Wonder dropped her head and sniffed the water, then looked at Holly, who had waded to the center of the stream. Holly nickered. Wonder made up her mind and tentatively stepped farther out.

Scooping up a handful of water, Ashleigh dribbled it over Wonder's back. "Feels good, doesn't it?" Caroline was gazing up the stream, lost in a daydream. Ashleigh felt a tingle of mischief. She skimmed her hand across the water and sent a splash in her sister's direction.

"Hey!" Caroline cried, looking down at her now-drenched shirt. Then she giggled and whacked a splash back at Ashleigh, getting Wonder in the process. The filly shook herself, then seemed to realize this was a game. She charged deeper into the stream. Soon a full-fledged water fight was in progress.

By the time they climbed out, they were all dripping, horses included. Ashleigh knew that Wonder wouldn't stray far from Holly, so she let the foal loose. She sat down in the sun next to Caroline, while Rory continued riding his pony up and down the stream bank.

"That was fun!" Ashleigh sighed, breaking off a blade of grass and chewing on it.

"Yeah, it was," Caroline agreed. She'd taken a comb from her pocket and was working it through the tangles in her wet hair.

Ashleigh looked out to where Wonder was grazing beside Holly, looking like a miniature version of her mother. They made a beautiful picture with the sun glinting off their copper coats. The creep feeding seemed to be helping Wonder grow faster. She was starting to fill out and grow into her long legs. But Ashleigh knew Wonder still hadn't caught up with the other foals. They were all still bigger and more mature. She had the feeling that Mr. Townsend wouldn't be impressed yet.

"What do you think of her, Caroline?" she asked.

"Wonder?" Caroline lifted her shoulders, then

winced as her comb hit a snarl. "She looks better than she did."

"I know, but will she be good enough for Mr. Townsend?"

"She's really cute and all, and I can see why you got attached to her. But maybe you ought to get interested in something besides horses."

Ashleigh thought for a minute. "I'm interested in other things. I just love horses best. What's wrong with that? You love clothes and rap music."

"You don't even look at boys."

"I look at them. Most of the boys in my class are jerks, and I'm taller than them anyway."

"You look like you've grown this summer, too." Caroline cast an eye over her sister's frame. "Still skinny and flat chested, though."

Ashleigh's cheeks flushed. She turned her head so Caro wouldn't notice, embarrassed by her scrutiny. "That's the best way to be for a jockey. I hope I stay like this."

"Are you kidding? You really want to be a jockey?" Her sister laughed. "You'll change your mind."

"No, I won't. When Wonder's old enough to go into training, I want to ride her. That's why I've been practicing so hard on Dominator."

"*If* Mr. Townsend decides to keep her."

Ashleigh frowned and looked at her sister.

"I hope he does keep her, Ash. I'm not saying that

he won't, but you ought to remember what Mom and Dad said about getting your hopes up too high."

Of course Ashleigh remembered. How could she forget? She thought about losing Wonder all the time, but she wasn't about to give up. "You just don't like horses enough to even understand how I feel," Ashleigh said stiffly.

"Sorry," Caroline said. "I wasn't trying to make you mad. Listen, why don't you come to the movies in Lexington with me tonight? I'm meeting Marcy, and Mom said she'd drive me in."

Ashleigh frowned again and tossed away the blade of grass she'd been chewing on. "Maybe. What's playing?"

"It's a comedy."

"Is it? Okay. I guess I'll come."

Later, when Ashleigh returned Holly and Wonder to their paddock, she saw Charlie approaching. When he had joined her, the two of them looked the horses over. "Wonder's looking better, isn't she?" Ashleigh said.

Charlie frowned. "Not bad," he said gruffly.

"What's wrong?" Ashleigh asked.

"Ah, Maddock has hired on a new assistant trainer —young guy. Can't be more than thirty. He's put him in charge of the two-year-olds still at the farm in training. Don't need him," Charlie grumbled. "Here I am just hanging around wasting my time. You'd think they'd let me do something worthwhile!"

"You're helping me with Wonder." It was the only thing she could think of to make Charlie feel better. "And maybe you could coach me on my riding when I take Dominator out."

"So you haven't given up on that idea of being an exercise rider?"

"No way!" Ashleigh exclaimed.

"Hmph," Charlie grouched. Then he dragged his hat over his forehead and, without another word, shuffled off.

Ashleigh watched him walk away, feeling hurt and confused. What was he trying to tell her? That she'd never make an exercise rider? First Caroline poking fun at her dreams—now Charlie. Didn't anybody understand how she felt? She stomped her foot. She wasn't going to give up her dreams for Wonder—and for herself. Wonder was going to grow into a beautiful animal and become a great racehorse. And Ashleigh was going to be good enough to ride her and help train her.

Ashleigh didn't see Charlie the next day, but when she went out to saddle up Dominator the morning after, Charlie was already in the paddock. He'd put a racing saddle on Dominator and was tightening the girth. He'd also put a regular English saddle on Belle.

Ashleigh stared, hardly believing her eyes, but she didn't dare question him. His mood didn't seem to have improved any, either.

"Guess I can still keep these old bones in a saddle," he said shortly. "But no fancy stuff for this mare and me. I've left your stirrups fairly long for the while. We'll shorten them when we get to that straight stretch, and you can gallop."

Ashleigh quickly swung up onto Dominator. Charlie *was* going to coach her after all! They set off at a walk. Charlie kept an eye on Ashleigh's seat in the saddle and barked out comments. "Keep your shoulders straight. Your weight's got to be balanced just right to help the horse. Time enough to lean forward when he's at a gallop."

Charlie pointed out other things as they trotted over the trails around the paddocks. "Your heels are sliding up. Keep 'em down, stretch out that calf muscle. Your reins are too slack. You don't want to be tugging on his mouth, but you don't want 'em dangling either. I know old Dominator's not going to go running off on you, but there's plenty of other horses who'd take advantage of that extra rein."

Later, as they came off the crest and were walking under the trees, a bird suddenly fluttered up from the brush beside Dominator. The horse was startled and shied sideways, nearly bumping into Charlie and Belle and almost throwing Ashleigh out of the saddle. Ashleigh quickly got him under control and soothed him with her voice.

But Charlie wasn't satisfied. "You weren't prepared for that, were you? Out on the track, you've got to be alert every second—prepared for anything, or you've got trouble!"

By the time they'd reached the long, straight stretch where Ashleigh did her gallops, she felt like a total failure. She'd thought she was a pretty good rider, but she sure didn't feel like one now!

Charlie saw her expression. "Don't take it so hard. You're good. I might even go so far as to say you're a natural. But if you ever want to get out there and win on a powerful, strong-headed Thoroughbred, with a dozen others pounding along next to you, then you've got to be better than good."

Charlie came to a halt and Ashleigh stopped beside him. "Take up your stirrup leathers a couple of notches," he said. "Jog him around a little till you get the feel of it. You're going to be balancing over his withers, and with the shorter stirrups, you're not going to be able to get your legs around him to balance that way. I'm going to ride up ahead. When I give you the signal, start him off. He's an old veteran. He'll jump right out. Gallop on past me to those trees up there, then start slowing him."

Ashleigh adjusted the stirrups. She'd never ridden with a racing saddle in a jockey's crouch before. She trotted Dominator in a few circles to get used to the feel of sitting so high with her knees tucked up almost to her chin. When she felt comfortable, she turned toward Charlie. He had pulled Belle up alongside the fence near the end of the straight stretch. Ashleigh readied herself. Charlie lifted his hand, then dropped it. Dominator needed no more than a tap of Ashleigh's heels and a cry of "Go!" from his rider.

He surged forward, his muscles bunching and stretching, driving him forward. His mane whipped in Ashleigh's face as she leaned close over his neck. She concentrated on keeping herself balanced, and allowed her arms and upper body to move in rhythm with the stretching motion of Dominator's neck. She felt much less secure in the racing saddle, but she was so engrossed in her ride that she didn't have time to be afraid.

She saw Charlie and Belle from the corner of her eye as she and Dominator flashed past. They pounded on until they passed the clump of trees, then Ashleigh began to slow the horse, straightening and leaning her weight away from his neck. The well-trained old Thoroughbred gradually dropped his speed.

Ashleigh turned him and rode back toward Charlie. She felt exhilarated, but she bit her lips nervously as she waited to hear what he had to say. He was frowning, but in a moment his creased face broke into a smile.

120

"We might just make an exercise rider out of you, little lady," he said.

Ashleigh grinned. She was on her way! One day she was going to ride Wonder.

She started going over to the training area every afternoon, talking to the grooms and exercise riders. She made friends with Jilly, the girl exercise rider. Jilly loved talking to Ashleigh about riding.

"When did you start?" Ashleigh asked as she and Jilly sat under the trees near the yearling stable block, cleaning tack.

"About two years ago, right after I got out of high school. I was a groom before that. Grooming's hard work, and you don't get paid much."

"But it's worth it if you love horses," Ashleigh said.

Jilly smiled. "Yeah, it's worth it. I'm going to try to qualify for my apprentice jockey's license this year."

"How do you do that?"

"Well, first you do a demonstration ride at a track. A track steward watches you break from the gate and ride about six furlongs. If the steward decides you're good enough, you can start riding in races as an apprentice. But then you've got to find a trainer who's willing to put you up on a horse so you can win some races and get your regular license. It's going to be tough. A lot of trainers don't think much of women jockeys."

"Don't you think Mr. Maddock will let you ride?"

"I think he'll give me a chance. He knows I'm good, and he wants winning riders. But there's a lot of competition."

"You'll do it," Ashleigh said. "I've seen how you ride."

"Thanks." Jilly smiled. "I'm going to the fall meet at Keeneland. I'll try to qualify then, so keep your fingers crossed for me."

"You bet! I'm hoping in a couple of years they'll let me exercise ride, too. Charlie thinks I'll be good enough."

"Well, just keep working at it, and don't let anyone discourage you, because they'll probably try."

Ashleigh frowned. "No, I won't let anyone discourage me."

In late August Linda came back from the New York tracks full of stories. Ashleigh was thrilled to see her. She'd really missed Linda over the summer. She'd gotten a letter from her and another from her old friend Mona, but it wasn't the same as talking face to face.

Linda couldn't wait to see Wonder, and the two girls hurried over to the paddock.

"Wow," Linda said. "She's really grown. She's filled out, too, and look at her go! She's keeping up with the other foals all right. She still looks kind of awkward, but she's holding her own."

Ashleigh let out a long sigh of relief. "I'm so glad you said that! I was afraid I was imagining things."

"Nope, you weren't."

"I just hope Mr. Townsend will change his mind."

"He's sure to, now."

"Nobody thinks so but me."

"And me!" Linda grinned.

Ashleigh returned the grin. "Boy, it's good to have you back! Let's go for a ride. I haven't shown you Dominator and Belle."

10

DURING THE NEXT WEEK MRS. GRIFFEN TOOK ASHLEIGH, CARO-
line, and Rory to the Lexington mall to shop for school
clothes. Only when Ashleigh was trying things on did
she realize how much she'd grown. She was a full size
bigger than she'd been last winter. She came out of the
dressing room to find her mother and sister waiting.

"I like that shirt," her mother said.

Caroline was more critical. "Why don't you get
something besides jeans? Look at this skirt I found. It
would match the shirt."

"I wouldn't wear it," Ashleigh said. "Jeans are more
comfortable."

"You could try it on," Mrs. Griffen suggested.

Ashleigh was feeling tired and irritable. She hated
trying on clothes. It was such a hassle, and they'd been
shopping for over three hours. She was thirsty and
getting a headache, and Caroline wasn't finished yet.

"I only want the jeans and shirts. I'll take Rory for a soda. He's got all his stuff."

Mrs. Griffen paid for Ashleigh's clothes, and Ashleigh took the bags and bore Rory off. "You know," Ashleigh said to Rory when they'd finished their sodas, "I think I saw a tack store down at the far end. Want to look around there?"

"Yeah," said Rory. So while Caroline and Mrs. Griffen finished their shopping, Ashleigh and Rory happily looked at saddles and bridles, riding outfits and boots.

"What are you staring at, Ashleigh?" Caroline asked. The two girls were in their bedroom doing homework. Caroline was at her desk, and Ashleigh sprawled across her bed. It was late September and, by seven, already dark.

Ashleigh jerked to attention. "Huh? Oh, nothing. I was just thinking. Dad's weaning the foals tomorrow. It'll be tough for Wonder. I want to get up early so I can be there."

"Then you'd better get to work," Caroline said. "You haven't written anything on that paper for at least fifteen minutes, and I saw some of your math papers. There were an awful lot of *D*'s, Ashleigh."

Overall, Ashleigh hated being back in school. It had been all right the first few days, seeing everyone again and hearing about their summers, finding out who her teachers were and who would be in her classes. But she missed the farm and the time she'd spent with Wonder and the other horses. The only thing that made school bearable for Ashleigh was Linda.

Homework was the worst, and she seemed to have so much more of it this year. She always put it off until after dinner, when it was getting too dark to be outside anyway.

Ashleigh turned her head and made a face at her sister. "Mind your own business!"

Caroline shrugged, closed her book, and picked up a teen magazine. "It's your funeral if you come home with a bad report card."

Ashleigh wasn't listening. She was wondering how Wonder would adjust to being taken away from Holly.

The next morning Ashleigh was out in the barn just after five. Her father had decided to wean six foals at a time. The foals could adjust to their separation from their mothers more easily if they were weaned with company, but it would still be a frightening experience.

Ashleigh talked soothingly to Holly and Wonder as she led them outside. But before they reached the big paddock, April walked over, took Holly's lead, and firmly led the mare away.

It didn't take Holly long to realize her foal wasn't with her. She looked back over her shoulder and whinnied. April held tight to the lead and urged the mare forward, and Ashleigh quickly turned and led Wonder toward a smaller paddock.

Wonder let out a cry and tried to pull away. The filly couldn't understand what was happening. Why were they taking her mother to another paddock? Ashleigh gripped the lead rope with both hands, trying to hold Wonder. The filly was as tall as Ashleigh now, and growing stronger every day—even if she hadn't caught up with the other foals yet. It was all Ashleigh could do to pull Wonder into the paddock and close the gate.

"It's going to be okay, Wonder. Easy, girl." Ashleigh tried her best to comfort the filly, but Wonder wasn't listening. She jerked on her lead, her eyes rolling in alarm. She dragged Ashleigh toward the fence nearest the mares' paddock.

The other foals were whinnying in a shrill and frantic chorus. They were gathered at the fence, pressing their bodies against it and trying to get through. Their cries only made Wonder more panicky.

Ashleigh knew she wouldn't be able to quiet Wonder yet. She unclipped Wonder's lead, then quickly moved out of the way as the filly charged off to join the other weanlings racing up and down along the fence. Wonder had only one thing on her mind—getting to Holly.

Two of the other foals started tearing around the paddock in panic, looking for a way out, and Ashleigh carefully stayed clear of them. They were nearly half grown now and could easily have trampled her.

Ashleigh watched Wonder anxiously, understanding the filly's fear and confusion. She wanted desperately to help, but she knew the only thing she could do was wait until Wonder began to calm down on her own. The minutes seemed to drag past, but at last Wonder stopped her mad dash. She still clung to the fence, though, searching for Holly, answering Holly's calls. Ashleigh gradually moved close to her, then gently patted the filly's neck. "You'll be all right, Wonder. I'm here. No one's going to hurt you."

Wonder was so upset that for the first time she paid little attention to Ashleigh's gentle tones. Ashleigh persisted, talking to the filly, trying to distract her. Then, finally, Wonder began to listen. Her trust in the girl who'd helped to raise her made a difference. She shivered nervously and snorted, but her ears flicked in Ashleigh's direction.

The other foals were slowly calming down, too. They were confused and unhappy, but their cries weren't quite so frantic; they weren't rushing so madly to and fro. Several of them started playfully chasing each other around the paddock. Soon the others joined in, and Wonder looked in their direction. "Go on, girl," Ashleigh urged. "You're going to be fine."

The filly seemed uncertain. Ashleigh gave her an encouraging pat on the rump, and Wonder picked up her heels and trotted toward her companions. She looked back over her shoulder once or twice, but Ashleigh motioned her on, then watched with a proud smile as Wonder joined the play.

"So you're still babying that filly."

Ashleigh jumped to hear Brad Townsend's voice behind her.

"Everyone's calling her Ashleigh's Wonder, I hear," he said. "Ashleigh's *pet* would be more like it."

Ashleigh spun around to face him. "I'm not babying her. She knows how to take care of herself. You can see how much she's grown."

"She's still a runt. You know, my father's not even giving her an official name yet. When the registration papers are filed, she'll be 'Filly—Townsend Pride/Townsend Holly.' We're naming Three Foot's colt Townsend Prince."

"Big deal!" But Ashleigh felt the shock of his words. Not giving Wonder an official name was close to confirmation that they were going to send her filly to the yearling auctions after the first of the year.

But she wasn't going to take his comments without fighting back. "I hear your colt didn't do too well in his maiden races," she said innocently.

Brad flushed as her point hit home. "So, he had some bad luck. He'll come along. He'll be racing again next week at Keeneland."

"Maybe he'll manage to do better than *eighth* then."

With that, Ashleigh turned her back and quickly walked off. She'd gotten in the last word, but Brad's news had frightened her. Later that afternoon when she had put Wonder in her stall, she stood back and studied the filly, trying to see her as a stranger might—trying to be totally honest with herself. Bill had told her that Townsend usually sent more than half the yearlings to auction.

Yes, in comparison to the other foals, Wonder *was* small and immature. There was nothing Ashleigh could do to ignore the obvious fact that Wonder stood several inches shorter and still had a lot of growing to do. But Ashleigh could see the potential in Wonder. If she were allowed the time to grow, she'd be every bit as strong, as beautiful, and as graceful as the other foals her age. But Ashleigh knew that Wonder wouldn't look so great to someone looking for the best in the crop.

She felt depressed as she finished feeding her. "It's not your fault, Wonder," she said. "And I haven't given up yet."

To keep herself from worrying, Ashleigh went over to watch the yearlings receive their first training. She'd probably see Charlie there, too, and maybe he'd have some encouraging words for her.

She saw him standing just inside the yearling walking ring and joined him.

131

"Watching this'll be good training for you if you're so set on being an exercise rider," he said. "And you'll see what's in store for that filly of yours if she stays on the farm."

Unlike the training oval, the ring was surrounded by high board fences that prevented the yearlings from being distracted by outside sights and sounds.

In the center of the ring one colt was being circled at the end of a long line attached to his halter. "That's a longe line," Charlie explained. "It's the first step in training. You get the horse going in a circle around you. You start him at a walk, then work up to a trot and canter by letting out the line. It helps smooth his gait and teaches him to start obeying hand and voice commands. When he's working out nicely, you longe him with a bridle, and then let him get used to a saddle on his back. After that you get him used to a rider. You usually do that in a quiet stall, though, a little at a time. Then you bring him back out to the ring and lead him around with the rider, like they're doing over there."

Ashleigh looked to where Charlie was pointing and saw a young horse and rider being led around the outside of the ring.

"You never want to rush a young horse. Just go nice and easy, and you won't have any trouble with them later on. And you make sure to reward them when

132

they've done a good job, so they're glad to do it again."

Ashleigh saw Jilly approaching. She was in the saddle of one of the yearlings being led to the walking ring. She smiled at Charlie and Ashleigh as she passed. Once she was inside the ring, the groom moved away from her horse's head, and Jilly picked up the reins. She quietly started her mount walking around the perimeter.

"That yearling's further along in the training," Charlie said. "He's already learned to obey the rider's commands. Once he gets used to walking and trotting in here, they'll take him out on the track and ride him alongside a quiet, mature horse, to get him used to the feel and look of the track. That'll be the end of his training this year. In the spring, when he's a two-year-old, the rest of the training work starts—getting him used to the gate, starting to breeze him."

"You think all of these yearlings will race next year?" Ashleigh asked.

"You've got to judge each horse on its own. Some horses aren't ready until they're three."

"Wonder will probably be one of the late ones."

"Maybe not," Charlie said. "I've seen a lot of foals born in May who were ready to race before February and March foals. Depends on the animal. I don't believe in racing them too early, anyway. Let's have a

133

look at that filly. You say she's learned to stick up for herself, eh?"

"She sure has. Even Three Foot's foal doesn't push her around."

"I hear they're calling him Townsend Prince," Charlie said.

Ashleigh snorted. "They haven't even given Wonder an official name. It makes me so mad. Brad thought it was a big joke that people are calling her Ashleigh's Wonder. He said she's still a runt."

"You'll just have to prove him wrong and make sure she lives up to her name."

They'd reached the weanling paddock. Ashleigh saw Wonder on the far side, grazing, and gave a sharp whistle. The filly immediately picked up her head, perked up her ears, and looked around. She saw Ashleigh by the fence and came trotting briskly toward her. She was tall enough now to easily reach her head over the fence. Ashleigh rubbed Wonder's nose, then fished in her pocket for a carrot.

Charlie studied the filly with keen eyes, especially when Wonder set off to play with some of the other weanlings.

He didn't say anything at first, and Ashleigh was dying to know what he thought. Finally he nodded. "Straight leg and a good thickness of bone, straight knees and cannons, a good angle to the pasterns. She's showing good muscle development in her chest and rump, has a deep girth and a flat and fairly short back."

"All of that's good?" Ashleigh asked.

"I can see the potential, but she's too young yet to tell for sure. Good conformation isn't everything. You can get a horse that's got perfect form but can't get out of its own way. She's a fighter, but she's still awfully small."

"Mr. Townsend's not going to be impressed, you mean."

"Well, he's got some other pretty outstanding foals. You gotta remember that this is a business. No owner or trainer's going to spend a lot of time and money on a chancy foal when he's got others that look like a sure thing."

11

"MY PARENTS ARE GOING TO BE MAD," ASHLEIGH MOANED TO Linda during the bus ride home. They'd gotten their first-quarter report cards that day. "I only got *C*'s and *C* minuses and a great big *D* in math!" Ashleigh didn't add that there was also a handwritten note from her math teacher saying she would fail if her work didn't improve drastically. "It's the worst report card I've ever had."

"Do you really think they'll yell?" Linda asked sympathetically. "I hardly ever get *B*'s, and my parents don't get upset."

"But you don't get *D*'s, either."

"No," Linda agreed.

Thankfully Caroline wasn't on the bus. Ashleigh knew her sister would ask her about her report card and want to see it. It was one thing telling Linda about it, but she didn't want Caroline to know. When

Ashleigh got home, she quickly changed, hid the disgusting piece of paper in the bottom of her drawer, and went out to the weanling barn. It was a cold day for late October, and most of the horses were inside. She hurried to Wonder's stall. The filly gave Ashleigh her usual cheerful greeting, but Ashleigh could only sigh unhappily in answer.

"It's not a good day, Wonder. My report card's so bad, I'm afraid to show it to my parents. What am I going to do? I know they'll tell me I can't spend as much time with you. Boy, do I wish I'd studied harder."

Wonder turned her head and nickered.

"Yeah, I'm in a mess all right. Maybe Mom and Dad will forget report cards are due?" Ashleigh knew that wasn't likely—not when Caroline and Rory would be bringing home report cards, too.

She was still debating what to do when Caroline came into the barn. "So how was your report card, Ash?"

"Never mind."

"Not very good, huh?"

"Oh, go away! And how'd you know?"

"Well, you hardly spend any time with your homework—you're always out here. And I saw the grades on some of your math papers. You weren't going to show Mom and Dad your report card, were you?"

"Yes I was," Ashleigh growled. "I just didn't feel like doing it now."

"Tell you what. If you switch off some baby-sitting days with me, I'll tell Mom and Dad I'll tutor you in math. Maybe they won't be so angry then."

"You don't even *pay* me when I watch Rory for you."

"Why should I? My tutoring's worth something."

Ashleigh glared at her sister. "I'll see."

Just before dinner Ashleigh talked to her parents. "You're not going to like this," she said as she handed over her grades.

"Ashleigh!" her mother exclaimed. "This is the worst you've ever done! Nearly failing math? Why didn't you tell us you were having trouble?"

"I didn't think my grade was so bad. I'll study harder—I promise!"

Her father scowled. "I wondered if you were spreading yourself too thin. The only solution is for you spend less time out in the barn. I'll get April to take over grooming Holly and Wonder, and no more rides on Dominator until you bring your grades up—especially math. And I want your homework done as soon as you get home from school—no going outside or hanging around the paddocks until I've checked it over."

"Oh, Dad, please, not Wonder, too!" Ashleigh cried.

Both her mother and father remained firm. "School

is important, Ashleigh," her mother said. "Right now horses may be the only thing that interests you, but even if you end up having a career with horses, you need a good education. Your father and I wouldn't be managing a breeding stable without one."

Ashleigh cringed. "I know. But it's been so different this year, trying to save Wonder."

"Wonder's safely past the stage where you have to worry about her survival," Mr. Griffen said.

"But I'm so afraid she's going to be sold!"

"We know you've gotten attached to her, but you have no control over whether she's sold or not—none of us does, except Clay Townsend. In fact, maybe it's time you became a little less attached to Wonder. I want you to buckle down and improve your grades. Maybe Caroline can help you with your math, or you can come to your mother or me if you have any problems. In the meantime, I'll tell April to add Wonder and Holly to her list."

Ashleigh felt stunned as she climbed the stairs. She couldn't believe her parents were doing this to her. She flung herself on the bed and buried her face in the pillow.

She was furious with her parents and depressed beyond belief. She hadn't felt this bad since they'd lost Edgardale. Sure, she should have spent more time on her homework, but did they have to take away Wonder? The worst part was her father saying she should become less attached to the filly. Had he given up hope that Wonder would stay on the farm?

"You can't let that happen!" Linda exclaimed the next day when Ashleigh told her about her parents' new rules. "It'll mess up everything!"

"I know," Ashleigh groaned.

"I've got an idea," Linda said. "I like math. How about if I help you during study halls? We can tell Mrs. Wilson what we're doing."

"Would you? I'd rather have you help me than Caroline, but I've got so much to catch up on."

From then on, every afternoon Ashleigh worked on her homework until her head ached. Linda's coaching in math helped, but Ashleigh knew she wasn't going to bring her grades up overnight. She missed all the hours she'd spent in the barns. That's where she was happiest. It was torture being stuck in the house during the few hours of winter daylight when she could have been with Wonder.

Ashleigh had to tell Charlie what had happened, since she couldn't ride Dominator anymore. She was embarrassed telling him that she'd let her grades slip so badly that she was being punished, but he smiled sympathetically.

"I never was crazy about school myself, but getting a good education's pretty important these days—more so than when I was a kid. You work at it. Old

Dominator will still be around when you get your grades up. And April will take good care of the filly."

"It won't be the same!"

"Things don't always go the way you want, but you hang in there."

At least Ashleigh could visit Wonder for a few minutes every night when her homework was done. April left her daily progress reports pinned to Wonder's stall door, since April was gone by the time Ashleigh could come out to the barn. April understood exactly how Ashleigh was feeling. If only Wonder could understand, too.

By early December, Ashleigh couldn't have felt much lower. The night air was cold, and there was a dusting of snow under Ashleigh's feet as she crossed the drive to the barn. Wonder whinnied with delight as soon as Ashleigh approached her stall, and Ashleigh hurried inside and threw her arms around the filly's neck.

"You miss me as much as I miss you," Ashleigh said in a choked voice as Wonder nuzzled her hair. "You don't understand why I don't take care of you anymore, do you? I haven't deserted you—really. I'd rather be with you than stuck in the house, but there's nothing I can do about it now except keep studying. I still love you."

The horse nudged her and grunted happily. Ashleigh laid her cheek against the soft warmth of Wonder's neck. At least the filly was still growing—that was one consolation. In another month, on January first, Wonder would officially be one year old, and she was beginning to look like a full-grown horse. She still had a lot of growing to do, but Ashleigh had measured her the day before, and she now stood fourteen hands at her shoulder—fifty-six inches. She was slowly catching up with the other weanlings, though Ashleigh knew too well that Wonder only had another month. Sometime in January Mr. Townsend and Mr. Maddock would inspect the newly turned yearlings and make decisions about which would go to auction.

The thought frightened her. She felt so helpless. "I know my next report card's going to be better, Wonder." She sighed. "And then I can take care of you again. Just keep eating and growing. It's important—for both of us."

Wonder bobbed her head, then touched her nose to Ashleigh's shoulder.

"I want to take care of you always. I'll just die if they send you to auction. But it'll be okay—I know it will. And I'm thinking about you all the time—even if I'm not here."

Wonder whoofed as if she agreed. Yet as soon as Ashleigh left the stall, Wonder hung her head and gave Ashleigh what seemed to be an accusing stare.

Ashleigh felt like her heart was breaking. She felt even worse a few days later when she came to the stall and saw April's note. "She's been off her feed. She's only eating half her ration. I wasn't sure whether to tell you or not, but I think she's not eating because she misses you. I'll tell your Dad about it."

Ashleigh crumpled the note in her hand and pressed her forehead miserably against Wonder's neck. This was exactly what she'd been afraid of. Here it was, nearly Christmas. She should be feeling happy and excited—not ready to cry!

She tried to talk to her father about Wonder the next day, but he was busy with a sick mare and didn't seem concerned about Wonder. "Their appetites go up and down, Ashleigh, and with the lousy weather we've been having, she hasn't gotten much exercise. She'll be fine."

Ashleigh was wakened by Rory's voice very early on Christmas morning. "Get up, Ashleigh, and see what Santa brought! There's a whole mess of presents!"

Ashleigh opened one eye and looked at her clock. "It's not even seven—and what were you doing downstairs? You know Mom and Dad told you to wake them first."

"I didn't open anything. I just looked. Come on! Get up!"

"Go in and get Mom and Dad," she told him. "I'll get Caroline up."

Within a few minutes the whole family had gathered in the living room around the tree.

"You think we should let Rory open his presents first," his father teased, "or should we make him wait till last?"

Rory gave his father a horrified look.

"I'm only joking. Go on, you first."

Rory scrambled over to the tree and tore into his pile of gifts. He opened them in record time. "Look, I got the truck I wanted! And a Ninja set. And a baseball bat! Santa got me almost everything on my list!" he cried.

"I guess you must have been a pretty good boy this year." His mother smiled. "Who's next?"

Caroline had crawled over to the tree and was already distributing presents. "This is for Ashleigh. One for me, and this is for Mom . . ."

Soon they all had a pile of presents in front of them. Most of Caroline's boxes contained clothing, and she was in ecstasy. When Ashleigh opened her own gifts, she found the two things she had wanted most—a new riding helmet and a pair of breeches!

"Thank you!" she cried. She ran to her parents and kissed them. She really hadn't expected that her parents would get her the riding gear she'd asked for. But when would she be able to use it?

By the time they were done opening gifts, the living room was strewn with wrapping paper and ribbon.

Ashleigh and Caroline cleaned up while Rory crawled around the room with his new truck and their parents went out to the kitchen to make a big Christmas breakfast.

Ashleigh still had Charlie's present to deliver, and she decided to do that after breakfast. The stable hands and riders who stayed on the farm for the holiday would be having a big Christmas dinner at the staff's quarters, compliments of Mr. Townsend. Charlie didn't have any family, so Ashleigh knew he'd be around. She knocked on his door and heard him shuffling over. He seemed really surprised to see her.

"Merry Christmas, Charlie!" She smiled, and handed him the brightly wrapped package.

"For me? Now what did you go and do that for?" But the old man's face flushed with pleasure.

"It's not much, but you've been so good to Wonder and helped me out and everything."

"That's real nice of you. It just so happens I found a little something around here with your name on it."

Ashleigh was amazed. She hadn't expected anything from Charlie. He picked up a slender, tissue-wrapped package from the table near the door. "Thought you might like this. I don't have any use for it anymore."

Ashleigh ripped away the tissue and discovered a jockey's whip. It was of beautifully tooled leather, and the initials C. B. were carved into the handle. She gasped with pleasure. "But this is yours!"

"Guess I didn't tell you that I used to be a jockey—a long time ago now. That's how I got started."

"Thank you! I'll take good care of it!"

"I know you will, and these handkerchiefs will come in handy, too."

On her way back to the house, Ashleigh stopped at the barn to visit Wonder. As she stepped inside, she saw Bill and Jesse and some of the other stable hands gathered in the barn office.

"Well, if it isn't Miss Santa Claus!" Jesse called out. "Do I get a stocking, too?"

The other hands in the office started chuckling.

"Ah, leave her alone," Bill said.

"But who ever heard of giving a Christmas stocking to a horse? Like the horse is going to know what's going on."

"I think it was a real generous thought," Bill said. "Where's your Christmas spirit?"

"I usually save my presents for people." Jesse laughed.

Ashleigh knew the teasing was in good fun. "Yeah, Jesse, what's wrong with it?" she called back.

"She's sure done a lot with that filly," one of the training grooms added.

But I'm not able to anymore, Ashleigh thought dismally, her smile fading as she walked down the barn aisle. She was sure Wonder was losing weight, and the filly wasn't as perky or lively. And as hard as Ashleigh had been studying, she'd only managed to bring her math grade up to a *C.* Her parents had told her that until she got her grade up to at least a *C*-plus, she wouldn't be able to take over caring for Wonder again.

On a cold Friday afternoon right after New Year's, Ashleigh finished her homework faster than usual. It was still light when she left the house for the barn.

As she came through the door, she stopped dead in her tracks. Mr. Townsend and Mr. Maddock were in one of the stalls, examining a yearling. The trainer had a clipboard in his hand and was busy making notes.

Ashleigh suddenly felt cold all over. She knew what they were doing—they were deciding which of the just-turned-yearlings would stay on the farm, and which would go to auction. And she knew, too, that Wonder wasn't looking her best!

The men moved on to another stall. Ashleigh could hear their comments. "Nice conformation, deep girth, well-angled pasterns. Let's hold on to this one."

Ashleigh stood frozen in place, her heart pounding, as they worked their way down the barn toward Wonder's stall. Two yearlings got raves. Another two weren't so lucky. In both cases Mr. Townsend said brusquely, "Put this one down for auction."

Then they went into Wonder's stall. As they'd done with the other yearlings, they felt Wonder's legs, ran their hands over her sides, checked her feet, and stood back and examined her from every angle.

Wonder was nervous and unhappy with the two strangers. She shied and snorted and tried to kick out as Mr. Maddock held her halter. Ashleigh wanted to run down the barn aisle and calm her, but she knew she couldn't interfere, and Wonder's show of spirit might be for the best.

"We almost lost this filly as a foal," Mr. Townsend remarked. "She was one of my biggest disappointments this year, considering her sire and dam. I had real high hopes for the match." He shook his head. "She's got some good points. Nice straight leg and strong forearm, a well-sprung rib cage, like her sire. She might have the same staying power with that lung capacity."

"She's immature," the trainer said. "Not nearly enough growth. She might turn into something eventually—but it could take a while. And would it be worth the wait? I seriously doubt she'd do any racing as a two-year-old. I see her as a real risk."

Ashleigh could hardly breathe, her throat felt so tight from fear—and anger, too, at Maddock's remarks.

Mr. Townsend was thoughtful, still undecided. "There's always the broodmare potential. Her dam's been a blue hen for me."

"That doesn't mean this filly's going to follow suit.

Derek Griffen would tell you the same. You could chance it, but it'll cost you more to bring her along than to sell her off as a yearling, especially if she turns out to be a dud. It's not worth it when you've got so many other outstanding yearlings."

Mr. Townsend scowled. Then he gave a quick nod. "Okay, let's put her down for the Keeneland Selected Yearling Auction. Let someone else take a chance on her. With her bloodlines, there ought to be a few takers."

Maddock made some notations on his clipboard, and the two men started to leave the stall.

Ashleigh didn't even think about what she was doing. She was furious. How could they decide Wonder's future so coldly? She raced down the barn to Wonder's stall and confronted the two men.

"No!" she cried. "You can't put her up for auction. You haven't given her a chance. You haven't seen how much she's improved. And she's got heart! She's going to be great—I know it! Please, give her more time."

Both men were astounded by Ashleigh's outburst. She was too frightened about Wonder's future to think about her manners, or that she'd interfered in something that was none of her business. But it *was* her business when Wonder was involved!

Mr. Townsend recovered first from his surprise. He looked down at Ashleigh's pleading face and suddenly seemed to remember who she was. "You're Griffen's daughter, aren't you? You're the one who nursed this filly?"

Ashleigh nodded.

He looked back to Wonder and frowned. "I have to say this filly's done better than I ever expected."

"She's doing better all the time, Mr. Townsend," Ashleigh pleaded. "It's just that she had so much catching up to do, especially after she got the flu when she was a few weeks old. And I'll keep taking care of her. It won't cost you anything—I mean, except for feed."

Mr. Townsend's lips twitched in a slight smile at Ashleigh's last words. Then he said, "So you think she's got heart?"

"Yes! I'm positive."

Mr. Maddock was shaking his head. "Filly's not worth taking the chance."

Mr. Townsend took another look at Wonder. "This farm is a business, not the humane society."

"I know," Ashleigh whispered. She closed her eyes for an instant, dreading what was coming next.

"I still don't know that this filly has any racing potential," he said after a long silence. "But I'll admit she's had a tough time of it. We'll give her another month. Let's see if you're right. Don't get your hopes up, though. If she doesn't look good then—she goes."

Ashleigh was too relieved and grateful to think of the negative possibilities. All she could do was gasp,

"Thank you, Mr. Townsend! You'll see a difference in a month—I know it!"

"I hope you're right." He motioned to the trainer and the two men went on to the next stall.

"I think you're making a mistake," Maddock said as they left.

Townsend shrugged. "What's another month?"

12

AFTER ASHLEIGH HAD CALMED WONDER DOWN, SHE RUSHED OFF in search of Charlie. She had to do something to save Wonder, and at the moment Charlie seemed the only one who could, or would, help. She found him in the training stables, passing the time of day with the grooms.

This time Ashleigh didn't wait for him to finish his conversation. She ran inside and waved frantically until Charlie saw her and walked over. "I can tell from your face that something's up."

Ashleigh quickly told him of how she'd confronted Mr. Townsend.

Charlie gave a deep laugh. "You've got guts, young lady, I'll tell you that. You could have had your head chewed off for interfering."

"But they were going to sell Wonder!"

"I know, I know." Charlie pushed his hat farther

back on his head. "I suppose you want to know if I've got any advice."

"Do you?" Ashleigh asked.

"You can't make that filly grow any faster than nature intended, but I know of a couple of things that might help. We can maybe improve on her feed, add a little more grain concentrate—not too much, though. Some breeders put yearlings on straight concentrates with no hay to fatten them up for auction. They'll grow faster all right, but all that fast growing isn't always so good for the animal. It can lead to bone and joint disease, and most of it turns to fat anyway, not muscle."

"It's bothered her, Charlie, that I haven't been able to take care of her. April says she's not eating well, and I can see the difference!"

The old man considered. "Your spending time with her is between you and your folks, not me."

"I know," Ashleigh groaned. "I've got to talk to my parents. It's so much more important now. But is there anything else you can think of to make her look good?"

"Well, what I was going to suggest is an exercise program, especially this time of year when the weather's too bad for the horses to be out in the paddocks much. They lose some of their fitness. What'll impress Townsend the most is her fitness, a well-muscled chest and hindquarters—a nice healthy look to her. I want you to walk her every day—long walks, not a couple of turns around the paddock. Take her up over the crest of the hill there, gradually build up the distance. You don't want to tire the filly—that'd do more harm than good—just keep her really fit. Of course that means you're going to have to go traipsing through snow and mud."

"But I don't know if my parents will let me!" Ashleigh was crestfallen. "I've got to finish my homework in the afternoon, and it gets dark so early now . . ."

Charlie pulled off his hat, toyed with it for a minute, and put it back on his head. "Well, let's go over and talk to your father about the diet, anyway." He scowled. "You been bringing your grades up?"

"Yes, but I still only got a *C* in math on my last report card, and my parents said I have to get a *C*-plus before I can take care of Wonder again."

"Hmph. Math hard, is it?"

"Really hard, but I've been trying! You know how much I want to be out in the stables and take care of Wonder."

Charlie thought for a minute. "You tell your father what you just told me, and I'll back you up."

They found Ashleigh's father in one of the stalls, looking over a mare who'd pulled a tendon. He smiled when he saw his daughter. "I hear you had a talk with Mr. Townsend."

Ashleigh flushed. She should have known how quickly the news would spread around the farm.

But to Ashleigh's amazement, her father wasn't angry at what she'd done. In fact, he almost seemed proud that she'd fought for the filly.

He listened to what Charlie had to say about the diet and nodded. "A small increase in the feed ration shouldn't hurt her," he agreed. "I'll mark her chart."

"But Dad, there's something even more important!" Ashleigh hesitated nervously, looked down at her feet, then up at her father. "Charlie thinks it would be a good idea to give Wonder *lots* of exercise. And Wonder hasn't been eating the way she should. April told me that she thinks Wonder misses me. And I miss her! I really think she'd be better if we could just be together again. Do you think, just for the next month, that I could take her out for walks first, then do my homework? I'd show it to you every night, so you'd know I got it done!"

He frowned. "Somehow I expected that question. I'll have to talk it over with your mother. I'll let you know."

Her parents didn't give her their decision until the dishes were cleaned up and Caroline and Rory had gone to the living room to watch television.

"Your father told me about what happened this afternoon," her mother said. "I know how you feel about Wonder being sent to auction. But I'm concerned about school, too. You put all your concentration and energy into that horse, and I don't want a repeat of what happened before."

"But Wonder's getting punished as much as I am!" Ashleigh cried. "She's not eating—she just hangs around her stall, moping. She doesn't understand why I don't take care of her anymore. Why should she be sent off to an auction just because I'm not there? And another owner wouldn't understand. They wouldn't know what was wrong—"

"Hold on, Ashleigh," her father said. "We haven't said you can't do it."

"You haven't?"

"I've noticed the change in the filly, too. And we've also noticed that you've been working hard with your homework. We set the C-plus limit because we suspected you wouldn't learn a lesson unless the punishment was pretty tough."

Her mother reached over and took Ashleigh's hand. "We're horse people. I understand how important keeping Wonder on the farm is to you. I would have felt exactly the same when I was your age. And Wonder is special, isn't she? She's tried so hard. None of us wants her to be sold. But in a situation like we're in right now, where we don't own the farm and don't have final say, she might be sold. We wanted you to try to break away from the filly, so you wouldn't be hurt."

157

"How could I do that?" Ashleigh cried.

"We've decided you can work with her this month. But no slacking off with your schoolwork. We still want to see your homework every night, and we expect you to do a good job."

Ashleigh had been so sure their answer would be no that at first their words didn't sink in. Slowly they did. She stared at both her parents, then her face lit up. "Thank you—thank you so much!"

But again, her father had a word of warning. "Just remember that there are no guarantees, Ashleigh. You can work your heart out, but you can't make Wonder grow faster than she's intended. Townsend still may decide to let her go."

"I know, Dad. But I've got to try."

"And that attitude is why we've decided to let you do this."

Ashleigh had never worked so hard in her life. Every morning before school she fed and groomed Wonder and mucked out her stall. Right after school, except when it was snowing or pouring down rain, she took Wonder out. She dressed herself in boots and a warm parka, and Wonder in a blanket against the chill. The two of them slogged up the trails around the paddocks. On most days the going was pretty tough—slush, snow, frozen ground, or mud.

Wonder loved being out of the barn, but she didn't

like the snow and slush at first. She'd never seen this white stuff before and wasn't eager to go trudging through it.

"This is important, Wonder," Ashleigh coaxed. "You don't know how important! You don't want Mr. Townsend to sell you, do you? We'd never see each other again, and who knows how they'd treat you? They sure wouldn't love you the way I do. If we're going to stay together, you have to build up every muscle and impress Mr. Townsend."

The filly stared at Ashleigh with big eyes. Her ears were pricked forward, and she seemed to understand the compelling tone in Ashleigh's voice. She whickered softly and touched her nose to Ashleigh's shoulder, then followed her friend out into the snow without protest.

It was only the ice that Ashleigh was afraid of. She couldn't risk the filly slipping or falling, and she carefully chose the ground where they walked.

Day after day they trudged uphill and down, covering first one mile, then two, then three. Often they returned to the dark barn, wet and dirty and cold, and Ashleigh spent an extra hour cleaning Wonder, making sure she was dry and warm before she went into her stall for the night.

But now that Ashleigh was caring for her again, Wonder started eating, and she no longer sulked in her stall.

April ran up to Ashleigh one afternoon, grinning. "She's licking her feed bucket clean." April laughed. "Good sign! She's not going to be sold if we can help it."

Linda was just as encouraging, though Ashleigh didn't get much time to see her friend except at school. Linda did come over one afternoon to plod along with Ashleigh and Wonder on their daily trek. "This is work," Linda said when they got back to the barn. "We just jogged five miles in the mud!"

"I know." Ashleigh sighed. "Fun, isn't it?"

Afterward, Ashleigh went to the house and sat down with her books. She was so exhausted. She wasn't taking as good care of herself as she was Wonder, and it was catching up with her. She barely had the energy to put on her pajamas. Crawling into bed, her head fell onto the pillow, and she was out.

The next morning she woke up with a sore throat, watery eyes, and a stuffy nose.

She hid her symptoms well, forcing herself through the school day, but she was shivering by the time she finished walking Wonder after school. Her mother noticed Ashleigh's flushed cheeks at dinner that night.

"Are you coming down with a cold, Ashleigh?" she asked.

Ashleigh wasn't about to let her mother know how rotten she really felt. "Just the sniffles."

Her mother put her hand on Ashleigh's forehead.

"You're burning up! Up to bed, now! I'll bring you some fruit juice and aspirin."

"Mom, I'm okay . . . really . . ." But Ashleigh's protests were weak. All she wanted to do was curl up in bed. She felt so cold. *By morning I'll be better*, she thought.

But she wasn't. Her fever raged. Her mother wouldn't let her out of bed. "But Wonder!" Ashleigh protested.

"We'll keep an eye on Wonder. You just rest."

Ashleigh agonized after her mother had left. How could she get sick now? It was the worst possible time! Every day was important. Soon Mr. Townsend would be coming to look at Wonder again. But even Ashleigh had to admit she felt too sick to get out of bed. She dozed off into fitful dreams.

"Ashleigh?"

Ashleigh dimly heard her name being called and opened her eyes. Caroline was standing beside her bed with a tray.

"I brought you some soup," Caroline said. "I thought you might be hungry. Mom says you've been sleeping all day."

Ashleigh pushed up on her elbows, and Caroline fluffed the pillows behind her, then put the tray on Ashleigh's lap. "How are you feeling?" Caroline asked.

"Not so hot," Ashleigh managed to croak. Her voice

sounded so strange! Ashleigh didn't feel hungry either, but she reached for the spoon. Caroline sat with her while she tried to eat.

"Linda called," Caroline said. "She wondered why you weren't in school and said she hoped you felt better."

"Tell her I said hi." Ashleigh had finished half the soup, but couldn't get another drop down her throat. She put down the spoon.

"Do you want anything else?" Caroline asked.

Ashleigh shook her head. She couldn't believe her sister was being so nice. "How's Wonder?"

"Okay, I guess. Mom and Dad are feeding her and stuff. They haven't come in for dinner yet."

Ashleigh leaned back against the pillows. Why did she have to feel so awful?

Caroline picked up the tray. "I'll see you later," she said.

Ashleigh dozed off again. She didn't remember much about the next two days except for her mother or father or Caroline coming by with medicine or food. But when she woke up on the third day, she didn't feel as shivery and achy.

Her mother came in with some juice. Ashleigh looked at the clock on the nightstand. It was nine. Caroline had already gone to school.

"Hi, Mom," Ashleigh said.

"It looks like you're feeling a little better." Her

mother smiled, handed her the juice, then went through her usual motherly routine, feeling Ashleigh's head, asking if her throat hurt. "I think the worst is over," she said. "A few more days in bed—"

"Days!" Ashleigh exclaimed.

"We'll see. You just rest for now."

Ashleigh tried. She napped for a while, then read her horse magazines. She forced herself to eat all the lunch her mother brought. Just after lunch Ashleigh looked up from her reading to see Charlie Burke standing in her bedroom doorway with his hat in his hands. "Hi, Charlie!" she exclaimed. "How come you're here?"

"I hear you haven't been feeling too good," he said as he came into the room and sat in the chair near Ashleigh's bed.

"I'm much better today," she said. Then she had a horrible thought. She sat bolt upright. "Something's wrong with Wonder."

"No, the filly's just fine. I thought you might be worrying, though."

"I have been worrying. She hasn't had her walks— and it won't be long before Mr. Townsend comes to see her—"

Charlie raised a hand. "Hold it right there. She's been getting her walks. If I wasn't so old and full of aches, I would have done it myself, but you've had some helpers. Your mother and that friend of yours have been taking her out."

"Linda? Mom? Why didn't anyone tell me?"

Charlie laughed. "I don't think you were in much shape to hear, missy. You've been pretty sick with the flu."

Ashleigh sighed, then frowned. "I sort of remember hearing Linda talking to me, but I thought I was dreaming. How does Wonder look, Charlie?" she asked eagerly.

"Fit as a fiddle. I checked her over yesterday and measured her. She's put on an inch or two at the shoulder in the last couple of months. A shade over fourteen hands now. She'll be full-grown before we know it. I don't think she'll be much more than fifteen and a half hands, but I've known plenty of good race-horses that size."

"You think the walking's doing her good? Do you think Mr. Townsend will change his mind?"

"Well, I can't say what Townsend's going to do, but I'd be impressed with how she's coming along. Don't you worry. Just get over this flu nonsense."

"I'm going to," Ashleigh said with determination.

Lying around in bed gave Ashleigh a lot of time to think. What if the worst *did* happen and Mr. Town-send decided to send Wonder to the auction? How much would someone pay for Wonder? Ashleigh had fifteen hundred dollars in her savings account. It was supposed to be for college, but maybe her parents would make an emergency exception?

When her father came up to see how she was doing, she asked him what price Wonder might bring.

"It's hard to tell for sure, Ashleigh. She's got good bloodlines, but some buyers might wonder why Townsend's putting one of Townsend Pride's fillies up for auction. I'd say she'd draw bids of five thousand dollars and up."

"Oh," Ashleigh moaned, "that much." Her hopes of buying Wonder herself had just been squished flatter than a pancake. And she knew without asking that her parents didn't have that kind of extra money.

"I know you're worried, Ashleigh, but worrying about it isn't going to help you get over this flu."

"I know, Dad."

That night she called Linda to thank her for helping with Wonder.

"But it was fun, Ash! I liked doing it, and Wonder's so neat. She really seems to understand what you're saying. She listens, and she tries so hard. I can't come over tomorrow, but I'll come over the next day, and I'll get some makeup work from your teachers. See you then."

After two more days in bed, Ashleigh had had it with being an invalid. She didn't care what anyone said. She had to see Wonder herself. After everyone left the house, she got dressed and went out to the barn.

When her mother saw her, she rushed over. "What are you doing outside?" she scolded. "Are you sure you're feeling well enough?"

"I feel great! Like I'd never been sick."

"The miracles of youth," her mother said. "I know you want to see how Wonder's doing. Just take it easy. An hour with Wonder, then back in the house to rest. I'll walk her for you."

"Thanks a lot for helping out, Mom."

Her mother dropped a kiss on Ashleigh's cheek. "You deserve it. And so does Wonder. We're a horse family, aren't we?"

Wonder gave a joyous whinny when Ashleigh stepped into her stall. Ashleigh rushed over to the horse and threw her arms around Wonder's neck. "Did you miss me as much as I missed you? I'm so glad to see you again! I've been so worried, but you do look good! Charlie was right. Oh, Wonder, I don't know what I'll do if Mr. Townsend decides to sell you."

The horse butted her head fondly against Ashleigh's shoulder.

"I love you, too," Ashleigh said.

Ashleigh spent a blissful hour with the filly. She carefully groomed Wonder, amazed to realize that Wonder's shoulder was now higher than her own. Then she sat down on the straw and talked to the horse. Wonder loved every minute of the attention and kept lowering her head to blow soft, affectionate breaths on Ashleigh's cheek. Ashleigh sighed in contentment and fed Wonder more carrots than she should have.

But when her mother came and told her to go up to the house, Ashleigh went willingly. She must have been sick if she felt this tired so fast.

By the time Linda arrived, Ashleigh was already feeling bored hanging around her bedroom. Linda plopped down on the bed and pulled out the makeup assignments for Ashleigh. "Your math teacher said to tell you that you're doing a good job."

"Did she?" Ashleigh was relieved, but she was thinking of Wonder. She'd just looked at the calendar and realized she only had a week left.

"They're having tryouts for the spring play tomorrow," Linda added. "I've decided to go."

"I'd be scared to death to get up in front of all those people," Ashleigh said.

"I may be, too." Linda laughed. "But it might be fun."

Before they started to work, Ashleigh told Linda how Charlie had measured Wonder, and how much the filly had grown. "Charlie thinks Mr. Townsend will notice how much she's improved. I went out to the barn for a little while this morning. She *does* look good, but I'm scared. Linda, I only have a week left until Mr. Townsend is supposed to come look at her!"

"You'll make it," Linda said. "Mr. Townsend will change his mind and keep her."

Ashleigh only wished she felt so sure. Was it all going to be for nothing? Was she going to lose something she loved—*again*?

13

ASHLEIGH HAD SPENT THE WHOLE MORNING WITH WONDER. First, she had carefully groomed the filly. She'd curried and brushed Wonder's copper coat, then wiped it with a soft cloth until it shone. Then she combed out the filly's silky mane and tail, and cleaned her hooves.

Now she stood back and inspected the horse. To Ashleigh's eyes, the filly looked gorgeous. Wonder's muscles were firm, and they rippled under her coat. Her finely shaped head was high, and her eyes were bright and alert. She gazed at Ashleigh with ears pricked and pranced across the stall to butt Ashleigh playfully with her head. There was no question that Wonder was now a fit and healthy animal. The only fault Ashleigh could find was that she was still small compared to the other yearlings. But there was nothing else Ashleigh could do. Now it was up to Mr. Townsend.

169

Ashleigh threw a light blanket over Wonder and kissed her velvety nose. "This is it, girl," she said anxiously. Wonder blew a soft breath against Ashleigh's cheek. "I love you, too." Ashleigh sighed.

She heard Mr. Townsend's voice at the end of the barn. She had almost hoped he'd forget all about the inspection and would just let Wonder stay in the barn. But he hadn't forgotten. Reluctantly Ashleigh left the stall with a final pat for Wonder.

She squeezed her hands together as she walked up the barn aisle. She was so anxious that her stomach hurt. She saw Mr. Maddock come inside with his clipboard in hand. As he opened the barn door, Ashleigh saw quite a few of the stable hands standing outside. Somehow word had gotten around the farm that Townsend would be making a decision about Wonder today. Charlie had told her that just about everyone was rooting for her and the filly. But that didn't mean much if Mr. Townsend didn't like Wonder.

When Ashleigh reached the adults, Mr. Townsend said briskly, "You've been working hard, I hear."

Ashleigh swallowed and nodded. "Yes, I have."

"Why don't you take her out in the yard and walk her around. We can get a better look at her out there."

Ashleigh was scared at the thought of leading Wonder around in front of all the watching eyes, but she was glad, too, that Mr. Townsend was going to do more than a stall inspection. He needed to see Wonder's movements, and Ashleigh knew that the filly would show better if she was leading her.

Ashleigh went back to Wonder's stall, clipped on the lead shank, and led the filly out into the aisle. "Okay, girl," she whispered to Wonder, "do your best." She felt dazed but determined as she brought Wonder down the barn. Her father had pulled open the barn doors, and a cold wind blew inside, but Ashleigh didn't feel the chill.

Mr. Townsend and Mr. Maddock had already gone out and were standing at the side of the yard to watch. Her father stopped her as she was about to step outside.

"Let's take off her blanket," he said. "No one's going to see her good points if she's covered up."

Ashleigh nodded mutely as he unbuckled the straps of the blanket and drew it off.

"She looks good, Ashleigh," he said. "You've done your best."

"Thanks, Dad," Ashleigh breathed. Her throat felt so tight, she couldn't raise her voice above a whisper.

Ashleigh took a deep breath, braced herself, and led Wonder forward. The filly hesitated as they entered the yard. Her ears shot forward, and she turned her head from side to side looking around. She sensed something important was going on. Snorting out anxious breaths, she pranced sideways on the end of her lead.

Ashleigh held the lead firm. "It's okay, girl," she said in her familiar soothing tones. "We're just going to go for a little walk like we do every day."

But Wonder saw all the people watching. She threw up her head and nearly pulled the lead shank from Ashleigh's hands. Ashleigh quickly tightened her grasp on the rope. "Easy, easy."

Ashleigh waited a second for the filly to quiet, then she led Wonder forward. She prayed that Wonder's show of spirit would impress the watchers. They certainly couldn't have any doubts that Wonder was alert and interested. "Come on, Wonder, come on. Show them you've got what it takes."

Wonder's ears pricked. She picked up her feet and followed along beside Ashleigh with brisk, clean strides. Ashleigh nervously led the horse up the graveled yard, then circled back toward the barn. She saw Charlie leaning on a paddock rail behind the others. He gave her a wink and a confident nod, and Ashleigh immediately began to feel better.

She saw Brad Townsend in the crowd, too. From the expression on his face, he was pretty surprised at Wonder's appearance—and impressed, despite himself. Ashleigh smiled with satisfaction, and led Wonder off in another big circle.

Mr. Townsend had only asked her to walk Wonder, but Ashleigh knew she had to do everything she could to show Wonder off. She picked up her pace and urged Wonder into a trot.

Wonder tossed her head but willingly followed her trusted friend. She arched her neck and elegantly lifted her feet, showing her best form. Ashleigh had to run to keep up with Wonder's long strides, but at a trot, the men could see the filly's smooth gait and the muscles flexing beneath her glossy coat.

Ashleigh thought she heard admiring murmurs from the people watching, but she wasn't sure. She was afraid to look at their faces. She brought Wonder around in another big circle.

Then she saw Mr. Townsend motion her to stop. She was so frightened, she felt dizzy. What was he thinking? She couldn't tell from his face.

She saw her parents, Caroline, and Rory watching anxiously from near the barn. Mr. Townsend and Mr. Maddock walked toward her. Neither of them was smiling.

Maybe Wonder hadn't done so well after all. If they decided not to keep Wonder, Ashleigh would just die.

Without saying anything to Ashleigh, they looked Wonder over. They felt her legs and rubbed their hands over her quivering muscles. Then Mr. Townsend walked away, turned, and studied Wonder from a distance of several yards.

Mr. Maddock joined him, and they spoke quietly together. Ashleigh couldn't hear what they were saying. For a second she had the strangest feeling that everything was blacking out. Then Wonder nickered and touched her shoulder, and Ashleigh came back to her senses.

Finally Mr. Townsend walked over to Ashleigh and smiled. "We'll keep her on," he said. "Another year, anyway."

Ashleigh felt dizzy again, but this time from pure happiness.

"I always appreciate hard work," he said. "You were right about this filly. She just might have something. You've done a good job with her, and I'd be hasty to send her to auction."

"Thank you!" Ashleigh gasped. She felt weak from relief and delight.

"Thank *you*," Townsend said. "I didn't really want to give up one of Townsend Pride's foals." He dropped a hand on Ashleigh's shoulder and gave her a quick wink. Then he motioned to the trainer, and the two men set off up the drive.

Ashleigh's knees were trembling so badly she could hardly stand, but her eyes were shining as she turned to Wonder and buried her face in Wonder's neck. "You're going to stay, girl! I'm so happy I could die!"

Her family came rushing over. Even Caroline seemed thrilled. "Congratulations!" they cried. "We're proud of you!"

"When I get bigger, I'm going to save a foal, too!" Rory exclaimed. "Just like you, Ash."

"Townsend was right about the job well done," her father added.

Ashleigh glanced over and saw Charlie still standing by the paddock. He gave her the high sign and called, "You're just beginning. Don't get soft yet!"

Ashleigh laughed. "All right, Charlie!" She knew she was just beginning—but she couldn't wait to get started on the rest of her plans for Wonder! The images danced in front of her eyes: Wonder in training, Wonder racing around the track with Ashleigh in the saddle, Wonder winning a race—the two of them proving to everyone that Wonder really was a spectacular horse!

"Now we can really dream, can't we, girl?" she said to the horse.

Wonder lifted her head high and let out a piercing whinny of joy.

Here's a sneak peek at what's ahead
in this exciting series:

THOROUGHBRED #2

Wonder's Promise

While they were eating, Ashleigh asked her parents
again about Wonder's training. "You really don't think
they'll let me help?"

Her father looked up. "No, sweetheart. They've got
professionals. You knew this was going to happen."

"But I know Wonder better than they do."

"That's true, but this is a business. Everyone on the
farm is impressed with what you've done for Wonder,
but from here on out they're looking at her as a
money-earning Thoroughbred—not a pet who needs
special attention."

"I don't think of her as just a pet!" Ashleigh cried. "I
want her to be a fantastic racehorse, too!"

"We know," her mother added. "But Mr. Maddock knows what he's doing—he's trained racehorses for a long time."

"He's turned the yearling training over to Jennings," Ashleigh said sulkily.

"I'm sure he knows what he's doing, too," her mother said.

Ashleigh was silent for the rest of the meal, but as soon as everyone was done, she excused herself. It was Caroline's night to clean up. "I'm going down to the stables."

"Just a minute, young lady," her father said. "You spent almost the whole weekend with Linda. What about homework?"

For once Ashleigh could smile about homework. "It's done. I finished it in study hall Friday."

"All right. Just remember what happened before."

How could Ashleigh forget being grounded for months because of her lousy grades? She hadn't even been allowed to take care of Wonder. She had no intention of that happening again! "I know, Dad, and I'm doing well this year—honest."

"I certainly hope so. Don't stay out there too late."

Ashleigh hurried outside. She'd been thinking of something all afternoon, since she'd watched the yearling training. It bothered her more than she'd thought that someone else would be in charge of Wonder's training. But there was one thing she was determined to do—and that was to be the first to sit on Wonder's back.

The barn was quiet. The horses had eaten and were dozing in their stalls. The staff had all gone to their quarters for the night. Before Ashleigh went to Wonder's stall, she collected a wooden stool that the grooms used to reach the higher shelves in the tack room. Wonder perked up and nickered as Ashleigh came to her stall door.

Ashleigh slipped into the stall. "Here, I've brought you some dessert," she said, giving Wonder some slices of apple. She ran her hand over Wonder's sleek back. "I think you're going to start your training soon," Ashleigh said.

The filly looked at her alertly, a soft, affectionate expression in her brown eyes, listening to Ashleigh's voice.

"We're going to try something new tonight," Ashleigh said. "You're going to have to get used to a saddle and someone sitting on your back pretty soon, and I think you'll feel better if I was the first one." Ashleigh hesitated. "Besides, I want to do *something* to help train you!"

Wonder nuzzled Ashleigh's palm and whoofed.

Ashleigh brought the stool into the stall. Wonder sniffed it inquisitively as Ashleigh set it down. "I just want you to get used to the weight of a rider," Ashleigh said. "All I'm going to do is lean over your back.

Okay?" Wonder continued watching and listening curiously. "You know I'd never hurt you. I just need to move the stool over next to you so I can stand on it." Ashleigh reached one hand around and moved the stool close to Wonder's side. Then she climbed up on it.

Wonder craned her head around and nudged Ashleigh with her nose. "Now I'm going to lean over your back." Ashleigh placed both her hands on the filly's smooth back. She pressed down slightly so Wonder could feel the weight. Wonder rippled her muscles but stood quietly. Ashleigh leaned farther forward, dropping her upper body over Wonder's back. The stool wobbled on the straw, and Ashleigh quickly straightened.

As she did, someone cleared his throat just outside the stall. Ashleigh froze, then looked over her shoulder. She let out a sigh of relief. "Oh, it's only you, Charlie."

"Lucky for you it is," the old man said. "If anyone else caught you trying to mount that filly—especially all by yourself in the barn—you'd be in for trouble!"

"Wonder wouldn't hurt me," Ashleigh said, patting the filly.

"Maybe not deliberately." Charlie scowled. "But she's not used to anyone hanging on her back, either. She could easily panic and throw you off. What're you trying to mount her for, anyway?"

"I wanted to get a head start on her training."

"They won't be breaking her to a rider for a while—not till she's doing okay on the longe line."

"I know, but I won't be able to help with that. I just thought it would be easier if I got her used to some of the stuff. Getting used to a rider will be her hardest part."

"Hmph. That's what they got trainers for," Charlie said gruffly. Then his tone softened slightly. "Well, if you're so determined, at least let me hold her for you."

As he unlatched the stall door, Ashleigh flashed him a big smile. "Thanks, Charlie."

"Don't thank me. I'm probably only helping you get yourself into trouble." Wonder nudged Charlie familiarly as he took hold of her halter and rubbed her ears. They were old friends. Charlie had helped Ashleigh nurse the filly through her influenza and had given Ashleigh advice about feeding and conditioning Wonder later on, when Mr. Townsend nearly decided to sell the undersized foal. For all he'd done, though, Charlie didn't like word of it getting around the farm. He told Ashleigh that the rest of the staff would think he was getting soft and sentimental.

"Okay," Charlie said, running his hand over Wonder's neck. "Go ahead and lean your weight on her. Easy, girl," he added to the filly.

Ashleigh added her own quiet reassurance. "It's just me, girl." Carefully she slid her arms across Wonder's back and lowered the weight of her upper body. For an instant Wonder snorted in surprise. She flicked her ears forward and sidestepped nervously.

Charlie held her. "Easy now, easy." He let Wonder turn her head so that she could see it was only Ashleigh. Then Ashleigh slid forward so that she was balanced over Wonder's back on her stomach. Wonder wasn't sure what to do. She didn't like having the weight on her back, but this was her trusted friend. She pranced sideways again. Charlie tried to soothe the filly, but her movement nearly unsettled Ashleigh. Charlie grabbed Ashleigh's leg and steadied her.

"You see what could have happened if you'd done this all by yourself?" he scolded. "You would have been right off and under her feet." He calmed the nervous filly, holding her in the center of the big stall, away from the walls.

Wonder rippled her muscles uneasily and snorted, then her ears flicked back as she heard Ashleigh's voice. "Good girl," Ashleigh said quietly. "You're such a good girl." Slowly Ashleigh reached up one arm and gripped Wonder's mane in her fingers. It didn't hurt the horse. When she was sure her grip was firm, she gathered her muscles, pulled herself up, and swung her leg over Wonder's back.

Wonder flinched in surprise and swung her hindquarters around, her rear feet dancing. "It's all right . . . it's okay," Ashleigh soothed. She saw that Charlie was glaring at her. He hadn't expected her to actually sit astride the filly. He shook his head, but concentrated on quieting the nervous horse.

Ashleigh leaned over Wonder's neck, rubbing her hand over the filly's silky coat, talking softly until Wonder slowly accepted Ashleigh's weight and finally stood still, ears flicking back and forth between Ashleigh and Charlie.

"That's enough for now," Charlie said in a moment. "Slide off her as quiet as you can."

Ashleigh did as he said. But once she had both feet firmly on the ground, she grinned broadly and went to Wonder's head. She dug a sugar cube out of her jeans pocket and fed it to the filly. "A special treat because you're such a good girl! You're terrific!"

The filly lipped up the sugar, then lifted her elegant head and nodded it decisively.

"Yeah, you know, don't you?" Ashleigh laughed. She threw her arms around Wonder's neck. "Isn't she great, Charlie?"

"You could've gotten yourself hurt," Charlie grumbled. "What if she'd reared up when you threw your leg over her?"

"She wouldn't have." Ashleigh beamed.

"You don't have enough sense to know when to be afraid," he grouched. "You haven't been around long enough to see the kind of stuff that can go wrong."

"But nothing went wrong!" Even Charlie's disapproval couldn't dim Ashleigh's spirits.

Finally Charlie relented a little. "Well, I suppose nothing did go wrong. But don't get any ideas about trying it again by yourself."

"I won't."

"Something I was going to tell you," Charlie added as he started toward the stall door. "Jennings is putting the filly in training tomorrow morning."

Ashleigh stared at Charlie, suddenly feeling a knot of panic clench her stomach. "He is?"

"Heard him talking to one of the training grooms about the schedule. You better be at the ring bright and early if you want to watch."

"But I have school tomorrow. I have to catch the bus as soon as I finish feeding Wonder!"

"I'll probably be around to keep an eye out." With that Charlie let himself out of the stall and headed out of the barn.

When he was gone, Ashleigh turned to Wonder. "Did you hear that, girl? You're going to start training."

Wonder nickered as Ashleigh laid her head against the filly's neck. Ashleigh felt a rising excitement bubbling through her. Tomorrow was going to be a big step for both of them. So much depended on Wonder's doing well in training and impressing the owner of the farm.